THE
FEATHER PROJECT

AN ANTHOLOGY OF SHORT STORIES

III

Copyright

Contents

The Nature of Heroes

By S.F. Lydon

Jak Owinsson stood upon the edge of the forest looking down on the military encampment below. He had finally made it. After two days of travel, he had found the camp of the Battlehawks; the most respected mercenary company in all of Kendar. He would finally be able to join the war and leave his boring farm life behind.

In his sixteen years of life, he had always dreamed of becoming a hero like the ones from the stories. So far, it has been an uninspiring beginning. On his two days of walking from Harnan Vale, he had encountered no bandits, no damsels in distress, not even so much as a wagon stuck in the road to start Jak on his way to herodom. But, then again, he supposed not every story had to begin with epic action and auspicious signs. At the very least he had left Harnan Vale and Erryl Crick far behind.

Not that there was anything wrong with either place, Jak supposed. It was all fine for men like his father, simple men with simple goals in simple lives. Men who wanted nothing more out of life than a farm and a family. Well, anyone who wanted such a life was welcome to it, but Jak meant to be something more. Something special.

All his life, Jak had been the biggest strongest boy in Erryl Crick, maybe even all of Harnan Vale. He routinely beat the other boys in wrestling and sparring with sticks. Even if they were not much in the way of competition, he had still shown himself to be worth more than a simple back country life. He could feel it in himself, something great waiting to come out. He knew deep down he was meant to be like one of the great stories. Maybe even as great as Cedric the Charmer himself.

And true, in all likelihood, he would not marry a princess or some high lady, but it would certainly still be better than what waited for him in Erryl Crick. His mother had had her heart set on him marrying Ethel Cooper from Tares Hill, farther up the valley. Now, Ethel was nice enough, but she was gangly as a stick figure and had hair like straw. Jak had had enough of straw for his lifetime. Plus, her teeth were crooked. No, he knew he could do better; especially once he made a name for the bards to sing.

Jak started down the hillside toward the camp. Green and white tents sat in rigid, precise lines in the fields around the hilltop that sat across from the fords of the river Wendle. A palisade surrounded the larger tents on top of the hill. Likely, that was where the officers of the company had set their command. Earthen works and a long ditch protected the rest of the camp. Open spaces were visible between sections of tents where men could gather and practice the arts of war. Jak could not wait to join them there and prove himself. He joined the line of men that stood out from the entrance to the camp; a slim bridge of earth over the ditch that led to a small breach in the earthen works. The whole point of the camp's position here was that this was the only place to cross the Wendle for almost twenty miles in either direction.

Jak stood there for what seemed like forever. Finally, he found himself standing before a small desk of oak, behind which sat a large man with a bored expression, writing in a large ledger. When Jak reached the front of the line, the large man barely glanced up before asking for his name and his credentials. Jak tried to be bold when he spoke but found he was stammering out something about Erryl Crick and this being his first time joining a military company. The man simply gestured to the open field to his left and muttered about presenting himself to the sergeant there.

Jak walked over, a little in awe of what was going on around him. This was a real military camp. These men were soldiers, hard men who fought for glory and loyalty and their own place in the stories.

He reached the field and his awe died quickly. There must be some mistake, the men, no *boys*, he saw around him were not the stuff of stories. They flailed around with wooden swords and blunt spears. They barely landed blows and the ones they did land were soft and almost listless.

This was not where Jak belonged.

After asking around a bit, Jak found the sergeant, a man called Baric. He presented himself to the man and tried to sound confident about it. He was dismissed almost immediately and told to join a group that had an odd number of trainees.

Jak joined the group he had been told to join and waited with the others. None of them seemed interested in talking. Half seemed too nervous to look anywhere but their feet; the other half stared around haughtily, as if everyone else were scum under their boots. Jak hoped he did not seem like either sort. In the stories, the heroes were always confident, but no aloof. Courteous, but not shy nor meek. He stood with his shoulders back and his hands tucked into his belt, doing his best to affect an air of confident placidity.

A man soon approached them. He was a tall, lean man, with a pointed black goatee and bored looking eyes. The man was named Sint. Jak was not sure if that was his first name or his last, but it seemed to suit him somehow. He spent as little time as he could explaining the exercises they were to perform, where to find their practice weapons, and how long they were to keep at it (until they were told to stop, as it turns out). After that he simply stalked off, his mouth twisting as if finally done with some unappealing chore.

When Sint was gone, one of the other boys finally spoke, "You all know who that was, right?" He looked around expectantly at the rest of them.

"Who?" Jak asked when no one else seemed likely to do it.

"Sour Sint," the other boy replied, staring back at Jak as though he expected the name to scare him. When Jak made no motion of recognition, the boy added, "He took four knights prisoner by himself at the battle of the Kriltop. Didn't even ransom them, just executed them after the fighting was done." He looked around with a leer on his face as if looking for a reaction to pounce on.

Two of the nervous looking boys paled at the mention of the act, and the first boy's leer grew. He looked as if he was going to say something new, but another boy spoke up. This boy was almost as tall as Jak, though much heavier and not with muscle.

"Enough," he said in a voice that was too high for such a large boy. "We had better get started or we'll have the sergeant to worry about."

After that, they went to one of the equipment wagons that ringed the field, donned their practice gear, and began to run through the drills. When the sergeant finally called an end to training for the day, Jak hated how relieved he was to find his assigned tent and sleep the night away.

The next week followed much the same pattern. A morning meal of hard bread and harder meat. Hours of training followed by another meal of hard bread and harder meat. More training followed until sundown, when they were allowed another meal of slightly softer bread and slightly better meat.

Jak learned more about his training mates over the course of the week. The first boy, whose name was Tef, turned out to not be as bad as he had seemed. Tef liked to talk, mostly of how his father had been a soldier and his destiny was to continue the family business of war. The fat boy, Mully, was nice enough and extremely focused on training. He worked as hard as anyone and after a week, he had lost a noticeable slice off his belly. One of the nervous boys was named Loring. He also had a father who had been a soldier, but unlike Tef, his father had hated war and raised his son to find another line of work. Unfortunately, Loring was not good at any of the trades he had tried, and finally, he had given in and joined the Battlehawks.

After a week of training, the wild swings and soft taps had turned into, if not precise, certainly more accurate jabs and hacks. Even the more reticent of the fighters was putting weight and effort into each swing. Jak still considered himself above most of these trainees, but he was no longer certain he was the best of them. Tef was a tenacious fighter and he would often leave bruises bone deep, whether he struck armor or not. Mully, despite being large and slow, was a patient fighter who waited for the right opportunity to land a heavy-handed blow that'll make a man's head ring for days. Even Loring proved himself capable of at least competency, though a lot of that had to do with the strategy of fighting that they were learning.

Jak had always thought of fighting as one man against another, a battle being made up of hundreds of these little fights. But what they were learning was different. They fought in pairs against pairs, each trainee paired with a shield mate. One would bear a large shield called a wall shield, while the other used a spear or sword from behind. The shield bearer would defend and the spearman would attack, when presented with an opportunity. The jabs and hacks they were taught were crude, if incredibly effective and easy to execute. It was not the picture of gracious sword fighting he had always pictured from the stories.

On the seventh day, Sergeant Baric began walking between groups of trainees, speaking to each of the trainees, and then moving on. When he reached Jak's group, he watched them drill for a few minutes before pointing to Jak, Mully, Tef and Loring and motioning them aside.

"You four," he began as soon as they were close enough to him, "are ready, or at least as ready as you're going to be. Report to Spear Company Four before dinner." Without waiting for a reply, he turned and strode off to the next group.

Jak hardly listened as the other boys began to talk excitedly as they walked off the training ground. This was it, the time for Jak to begin his real story. His own legend was beginning now.

They reported to their new commanding officer, a Lieutenant named Alric, He was a man of average height, average build and above average age. His face was craggy with wrinkles, the lower half covered by a hoary thatch of a beard.

The food here was better than the fare during training, and for once the boys were happy for more. After his second plate, Tef tapped Jak on the shoulder, jittery excitement lighting up his face. "Come on," he whispered. "You've got to see this."

Jak looked at Mully and Loring, wondering why Tef had singled him out. Loring was tucking into his third serving of dinner and Mully was half asleep over his mug of ale. Shrugging, Jak got up and followed Tef. They strode past the section where their company camped and toward the center of camp. They approached a campfire with a smaller circle sitting around it, but a large crowd standing around them. Jak wondered if there was some kind of fight or contest going on, but when he got closer he was even more surprised.

"Galen Greenspear!" Tef whispered again in his ear. Not that Jak needed to be told who this man was. Galen was seated across the fire from where they stood. He was a tall, well-built man, with long dark hair, flowing to his shoulders. His face was clean-shaven and his eyes glowed with merriment and confidence. This man was one of the most celebrated heroes of the last ten years. Jak had not even known that he was riding with the Battlehawks.

Next to him sat a dark-skinned man with a shaved head and two sword hilts sticking up over his shoulders. There was only one man in Kendar with that shade of skin; this had to be Toren Dal. The stories said Dal had the fastest sword in all the Southern Sands.

Jak mentioned this quietly to Tef, who nodded quickly and pointed to the man on the other side of Galen. "Lowen the Loser!" Jak noticed the lion engraved on the man's breastplate and knew Tef was right. Lowen was one of the most renowned knights in the land. Once he had been called Lowen the Lion, but his penchant for choosing the wrong side in any battle had overshadowed his own personal prowess.

Galen was in the middle of telling a tale when they arrived. As he approached the end, Jak realized it was the tale of Killian Kingkiller. A fine story about one of the best knights of the last half-century who had killed Crestor's, the current king, father, who had been a terrible despot. Of course, the story left out how that act of heroism had sparked the current war of succession between Crestor and his brother, Polac. A minor detail anyway.

Galen had just finished the tale with the usual line of "Killian, a true hero!" when another voice spoke up from the near side of the fire.

"A fine hero, and dead before thirty, like all those other *heroes*." Everyone turned their attention to the man, most of them sneering at his comment. It turned out the speaker was their own company Lieutenant, Alric. Galen did not seem at all put out by the interruption, however.

"Ah, Alric," he said almost condescendingly, "always the same stance on these tales. Always knocking brave men for their great deeds." He smiled around at the onlookers, as if indulging them in a shared joke.

"Its not the deeds I knock, it's the foolhardy ways they spend their lives in the doing of those deeds that I take issue with." Alric spoke well for such a ragged looking man. "All I mean is a little prudence would have served those men better than their eagerness to earn their place in history. I have no objection to bravery when it is called for, but foolishness will always earn my scorn."

Galen's smile slipped a bit at that. He seemed close to saying something biting in return, but instead, he smiled again. "Bravery when it is called for you say? And what would you know of bravery, Alric?" He looked around at the crowd again. "Alric here," he gestured to the bearded man, "had run from more fights than any man here!" The crowd burst into laughter at that, as Alric's face turned red.

"If I've run from so many fights its 'cause I've lived long enough to see so many." Alric said it simply, not as a retort, but a mere statement of fact. But Galen seized on the admission.

"He doesn't even deny that he runs when the battle turns against him!" Galen trumpeted, smiling broadly, though the smile no longer seemed so nice. If he expected Alric to back down, he was to be disappointed.

"Aye, I've run," Alric said, "when the battles were hopeless. All those heroes you love, they fought past the point of sense, past the point when the battle was unwinnable. All for a place in the songs." He glared around the fire daring a man to call him wrong. "But I've also stood when the fight was hard. I held the line with Toric the Elder and Younger Toric after him. I held it with Honig himself, before he was Headless." Some men around the fire were nodding along now, seeing the sense in what he said. Jak found it hard to disagree but he also had a hard time believing any of those heroes he had worshiped his whole life were fools.

"Yes, you held the line," admitted Galen, standing now to look down on Alric. "And here you are, still in the line, while all those better men went on to glory and now their names are sung across the land."

"Aye," said Alric, standing himself, though he still had to look up to meet Galen's eyes. "They went on. To glory and an early grave. Personally, I'd rather be late to mine." He stared at Galen for a beat before stalking off into the night.

Once Alric was gone, Galen and his entourage moved away as well and the onlookers were left to seek their beds. Jak and Tef went back to their own tent, neither saying a word. Jak was surprised by the pensive look on Tef's face. He'd never considered

Tef too much of a thinker. They hit their cots heavily, Mully and Loring already snoring away, and fell quickly into sleep.

The dawn came fast, and the trumpet call to arms came soon after. Jak and his tent mates donned their new armor, given to them the day before, and hurried to join the ranks as they assembled along the field between the ditch and the fords of the Wendle.

The ranks of Spear Company Four found themselves along the eastern edge of the ford. The enemy ranks were already marching toward the ford on the other side of the river. There were at least several thousand. The Battlehawks fielded almost two thousand foot soldiers and another five hundred cavaliers.

The cavalry would not be needed unless the shieldwall failed to hold the ford. This was unlikely. It was plain to Jak that they held the better ground. They were uphill and out of the water. The enemy would have to fight uphill in muddy ground after making their way across the unsteady footing of the ford.

The battle started faster than Jak had expected. The enemy simply came on despite the unfavorable field. Jak was several lines back of the front line. It would be some time after the first clash before his line was called forward to relieve the men in front of them. The sun was rising on their right as the two front lines met. Tef was several men down the line, Mully was directly to his right, with Loring on his left as his shield mate. It was difficult to see what was happening over the head high shields of the ranks in front of him.

Time seemed to pass strangely, one minute he was standing, almost bored, and the next his rank was being called forward. The horn sound for the rotation of men came loud across the morning air and they were thrust into the front line. The fighting was almost to the water line now. The ground was all churned mud now and the enemy were right there in front of him. He relied on his training, trusting his shield mate, waiting for his openings before stabbing out with his spear. The first time it came back red he almost retched. But he reminded himself this was war, fought down his gorge and willed his stomach to stillness.

Before Jak knew it, the horn call sounded and his turn was done for now. He rotated out and allowed himself to breathe. It was hard, trying to keep his spear out of his line of sight so he would not see the gore and blood on it. His turn came again and again as morning turned into afternoon. It was not the glorious warfare he had anticipated; it was more like butchery than anything else.

Suddenly, another horn call rang out, but it was not the Battlehawks horns. It came from the east. Orders rang out for the ranks to turn east, but Jak, in his inexperience, was caught between staying to face the enemy and turning with the others. Tef was suddenly beside him turning him east. Over the rise, a long line of heavy cavalry rode down on the invested infantry of the Battlehawks.

Chaos reigned. The infantry ranks shattered. Jak found himself standing amidst the thundering horses and dying men, wondering how he had ever wanted any of this.

A man standing next to him was spitted on a spear by a passing horseman, at an angle that pierced the ground and left him propped him up like a blood-covered scarecrow, his eyes goggling at the three feet of spear shaft sticking out of his stomach, the light slowly leaving them.

Jak ran.

He headed for the forest to the west. The forest that would hide him as he fled toward home. He could not fight it any longer. All he wanted was to go home. He dodged horses and men, occasionally swinging his spear or throwing up his shield to protect himself; but mostly he ran.

The thundering sound of hoofbeats sounded behind Jak, seeming to follow him no matter how he zigged and zagged. At last, he turned and threw up his shield, hoping to catch the oncoming blow.

But the blow never came. The horseman flashed past him and was gone; no spear in his hand. Jak lowered his shield to see Alric standing in front of him, a spearpoint standing out of his chest.

"R-run, boy. Run" Alric's rasped out before falling to his knees, dead eyes still staring at Jak. If it were not for the chaos and death around him, Jak would have kept staring at Alric's dead body, but he took the dead man's words to heart and turned to run again.

As he ran, he saw other horrible sights. Mully dead from several gaping wounds, Loring pierced with arrows, Tef trampled into the mud; hoofprints littered his back. He saw Galen atop his horse surrounded by pikemen who eventually pulled him down and he was lost in the mud and blood. Toren Dal fought several men at once with great skill, until a spear thrust through the knee hobbled him. He was dead seconds later. Lowen the Loser lay in the mud with blood pouring from beneath his helm. A glance over his shoulder showed the command tents on the hill being abandoned and a group of several hundred horsemen fleeing to the south.

Against all odds, Jak reached the edge of the woods, the exact spot he had been standing on when he first looked down on the camp. With a last look he turned and fled deeper into the trees.

As he ran, he thought about what Alric had said about heroes, coming to the conclusion that there were Heroes and heroes. Galen was a Hero. He died young and the songs would sing of his deeds. But were those deeds any greater than Alric's? Alric had saved his life. He was a hero. No songs would sing of that.

But Jak would always remember.

The only thing left to ponder, was what would Jak do now?

He would go home. Go home and become a farmer and live a simple life. Maybe even marry Ethel Cooper. After all, she wasn't bad looking. Sure, she was skinny, but strong too. He'd seen her hauling water enough times to know, hadn't he? Her hair was like straw but in the sunlight it glinted like gold, didn't it? And her teeth weren't crooked exactly. Not even, but still charming in their way.

Yes, he would go home and live a simple, safe life.

Cost Of Freedom

At what point do you know what fear truly is? And what I mean is, fear in all of its means and iterations. Terror, horror, dread, creep, anxiety, and all possible ways of describing one of living nature's most primal senses. Most attempts at understanding fear only go so far as to poorly replicate its effects by cheaply imitating its triggers. Drawn up pictures of grotesque beings, fiction written from the point of view of corrupted minds, numerical statistics of cancer likelihoods and death tolls.

Even as these come close to the true root of fear, many choose to walk free of them, the societal machination in which they are born in offering many avenues to turn away from their natural calls to the void. To them, fear stems from the pettiest of life's wants. Are they going to find love, a successful job, live a long life, understand the vast complexities of the universe? All basic things that make it seem that fear only stems from the absence of want.

These fears bore me. Nothing but another speck of dust in the very blowing dunes of existence to a collector such as myself. What someone like me is after are the fossils. The remains of the dead buried in life's blowing wind, their suffering forever memorialized in a set cast of their misery. Aren't they just the most magnificent things to behold? Pain woven right into the foundation of where we lie today…

My apologies, it seems that I've gotten ahead of myself again. I find it hard to contain myself when talking about such… visceral material. My position has allowed me ample time to find the beauty in decay, a fascination that I hope to share with you all now.

Because, understand this, suffering is an inspiration that many of us jerk and stray away from. It seems everyone now is far too eager to numb all of their senses, especially fear, for the minuscule net grain of pleasant contentment. You all don't get to see what I see. Feel the lifetimes that I have walked through. But now you will learn not only my name but what my own experiences have brought me. I'm here to awaken you, to widen your eyes, make you focus, and feel the pain all around you.

My name is Graven, and these are my accounts.

This was one of the first stories I collected, a fitting intro for my volumes. It's a personal tale, one of a young boy who simply wants some independence in his life. A coming of age story if you're an optimist or eyeless romantic. And like all inspiring stories, it blossoms from a dying prostitute in a crack house. In the arms of one Tyler Bindweed.

Before you go casting judgment on our young boy here, one must understand how hard it would be to be your own man at sixteen. But young Tyler was actually handling it well. Of course, the normal connotation of well is not exactly the best fit for the situation here. No one could be well after running away from their orphanage. Or having an abusive drunk father that threw more bottles than the number of times his checks bounced. Or having survived a religious nut mother tried to gore out the demon in their soul. No one could say anything was well in that scenario. The connotation of Tyler's entire life is needed to make sense of all this senselessness and for that, one has to start at the very beginning.

Tyler had never felt truly free. From his birth, he felt controlled. His cage was the clogged up heartland of the American east coast, Kentucky bluegrass country, the sentencing date being April 13th, 1973. It was directly from the maternal womb of his mother to the whipping belt of his father. What had once been a hard-working family man was now a violent drunk. The long-standing family business was going under and his father was handling it about as well as he did apple pie moonshine. A man at his kind of low point just wants to put hurt out into the world, and too often Tyler was the closest outlet. That was only because the mother was out bible thumping.

Carrying Tyler had been a labor of love for his mother starting out. Then by month eight it had turned into a labor of unspeakable anguish. Tyler was a late arrival and his actual delivery was difficult. To come out of all of that to return to a crumbling home and drunk husband, reasonable to see why she went as mad as she did.

Her sudden discovery and devotion to Christ from a dream was considerably less so. Her rare atheist upbringing made it all the more special and unhinged. But when the ground below your feet falls away, there's only one place to look toward and that's up into the sky. And people love pulling things out of clouds.

The clouds seemed to have told her to start badgering her neighbors and calling her only son a relative of Satan. The reason for all of the family's troubles. A burden put on earth for her by God to test her newly found faith. Parents usually put a lot on their kids though so that was par for the course.

This all came to a head when the father was somehow even more sloppy with his drunken beating and hit Tyler in the face. One good shiner was all that was needed to confirm the long-held suspicions of Tyler's school teachers. Soon Tyler was pulled aside, interrogated, and put in a little safe room while the teachers called the police. They had always worried for Tyler, his more-than-quiet behavior and odd ticks were a point of concern between them. Now their nativity was leading them to believe that local authorities would be enough to stop the anguish of this poor boy. It would soon turn out to be the subtle flap of the universe's butterfly wings.

The cruiser pulled up to the lonesome house, not even bothering to see if anyone else was around the property. The two cops on patrol that day were very aware of the Bindweed family, their father causing more than enough scuffles in the town bar to warrant his own corner in the stations holding cell. They expected the father to be out on his ass drunk watching something on T.V., an easy arrest. However, by the time the officer had arrived, the school was already let out. That meant Tyler should have been home. His father was not one to miss out on time spent with his favorite punching bag, so he knew something was up. The sound of car tires pulling up on the dirt road was all he needed to get out his shotgun.

The police sauntered up the dilapidated porch, not prepared for the double-barreled welcome waiting for them. They were chuckling to themselves, taking guesses at what slurred excuse the father would have for them this day. It was their own snickering that covered up the sound of two shells being loaded into the father's break action. The senior officer's knock was the opening sting to the orchestra of buckshot being fired through the door and into the policeman.

His partner, deafened and stunned at the sight of his mentor being torn apart like apple mash, stumbled out of the way of the second spread of red hot pellets. The father's aim, unlike his paranoia or rage, was not helped with whiskey. Neither was his footing, as the father tripped over himself trying to swing his spent weapon at the remaining officer. The opening let the remaining officer take out his revolver and fire right into the father's chest, followed by three more as the rabid drunk's body dropped to the ground. As the downed man's blood seeped into the rotting poach wood, he reeled thinking he had ended the evil of the damned home.

A returning matriarch would cut short any chance of closure. She was right outside, returning from yet another failed conversion session when her new reality soon hit her. Instead of the usual treat of another bill taped to the front of the home, what was there was her deadbeat husband, truly dead and beaten. One in the shoes of a long-abused wife might find this sight horrifying yet relieving to a certain extent. Yet this woman had one thing she hated more than her drunk and now dead husband: Police.

Men and women acting as the arms of a long and corrupt creature of sin. Just the mere sighting of one meant that more godless creatures would come into her home. It would be like a plague. One that could have only been brought on by a wicked curse. One that was created inside of her. One who too conveniently did not seem to be there at the house at the very moment.

If the policeman thought seeing his partner get shot was the low point of the day, I'm sure having his cruiser jacked by a screaming lunatic of a woman was at least the strangest one.

The mother peeled away from the house, determined to rid the world of her own perceived demon. Meanwhile, the secretary leaving Tyler's school was probably just determined to call a plumber to finally fix that leaky pipe under her sink. It would be the secretary leaking out on the pavement after the mother arrived and plunged her dagger deep into her chest. That sacred dagger mimicking the spearhead that stabbed Jesus finding its way into the chest of a secretary called Mary. What was once a powerful example for the mother to pull out and show others the personal sacrifice Jesus had made for humanity, now a great image of irony.

Those teachers witnessing said stabbing probably didn't have the clairvoyance to appreciate the coincidence however. The mother hadn't any mind for it either as she broke through the front door of the office. Her eyes snapped toward and her feet stomped right over to her terrified little hellspawn. Tyler was in the back of the room, chair facing what was sure to be his death. But as the mother made her charge toward Tyler, the football coach of the school had come up from behind and tackled her to the ground. Soon everyone rushed to dogpile on the crazy mother who was now screaming and flailing around, all the while in a locked stare down with her boy. Her bloodstained face and howls forever etching themselves in the heart of Tyler.

Was it any wonder why then after all of the death and screaming and demon-labeling that the kid didn't turn out to be quite the talkative type? Tyler became a practical mute after the incident, the entire country soon being made aware of this crazy family. The people ate it up. The perfect American town turned upside down. Nothing gets the masses more wound up from the comfort of their couches and air conditioning. Tyler, on the other hand, was being passed around from psych office to psych office, any therapist worth his salt wanting the fame of helping the most troubled boy in all of America. But Tyler was clam, not even offering so much as a crayon drawing to show the things he was put through. The world asking for your story when all you want to do is to try and process it all is a tough thing. Eventually he was shipped off to some orphanage on the other side of the state. Some people realized all the microphones and cameras might hurt the poor boy's mind. But trying to save it was a lost cause.

Tyler was once again thrust into a horror house with strangers that should have been caring for him but instead were just causing him pain. So, he decided to fall back on what his dad had taught him best to do. Run. Run and hide. In the dead of night, he escaped the orphanage and just ran with some granola bars and water bottles all to his name, carrying in the same backpack he had when his mother tried to kill him.

The next morning, of course, there was another roundabout the news circuit on the disappearance of America's favorite trauma boy. There were search parties sent around the area, though the local police were well and truly tired of this whole Tyler fiasco. Still, they tried with some measurable amount of effort to find him but to no avail. But it was because he was not in the town dumpster or lost in the woods huddled in a cave somewhere as everyone presumed. Tyler was in a long thought abandoned house full of local drug addicts and dealers.

The '70s were a great time to deal heroin. It was as popular M*A*S*H. Even with the colorful characters drugs usually tend to attract, it can be said with certainty that the people dealing heroin did not expect a 10-year-old boy to show up on their doorstep. Tyler had only come there because it was the only place the caretakers at the orphanage told him not to go. Installing the fear of a creepy and decrepit house would have probably worked on any other child. Home didn't carry the friendly and inviting connotation in Tyler's mind so busted out windows and dangerous people were just par for the course. He knew it'd be the last place anyone would look for him so it was a fantasy land in his eyes. All he had to offer, however, was his hands for work and some of his stolen granola bars. Thankfully the happy heroin dealers took him, mostly because they were high at the time and thought it would be cool to have a "celebrity" in their dilapidated home.

So for the next five years, Tyler's life was that old home. He started out as just a lookout for the dealers. He was still a mute at this point, so he carried around an old cowbell as an alarm. That soon became his calling card among the dredges of the town, calling

Tyler the name Bell instead of his own. He didn't mind of course. If anything it was another thing that put him away from his past. He would be Bell and that would be it. No more questions. No more demands. No more family ties besides the nightmares in his head.

But he would see a whole lot of other family troubles. In the ever disintegrating shack he now called home, the dealers would bring in buyers to "sample" products. These interested investors ranged all over the moral spectrum. Some defunct workers from local coal unions faced the hardest of hard times while others were widowed wives seeking an escape from all of life's troubles. And some were just completely corrupted shitbags you could not believe were once human.

It's why Tyler would never touch the product. Despite the near-constant egging on from his dealer counterparts, Tyler would simply shake his head at any pass of the needle. Same thing for liquor or marijuana. His dad would say he drank to change, to get rid of all the pain in his life. Tyler had seen that experiment fail in front of his eyes. He figured people were just meant to carry heavyweights in their hearts. Just like himself, everyone in the house had already given up and was beyond redemption in their own eyes.

But one always stood out to Tyler: An older girl in her 20's, who was simply called Tink. That's because whenever she was high any can or light metal object would be subject to her finger pecking. That sound was the only thing she would make when she was strung out. Soon one day when Tyler was just hanging around, Tink got a good look at his bell and fell in love. At least when she was strung out. And Tyler didn't mind because Tink, even whacked out of her mind, was easy on his eyes. Plus she never asked questions unlike everyone else. It was just about the only relationship Tyler could ever think of having long since given up facing the general public. He didn't care if she was a prostitute or higher than a weather balloon. It was nice for the two months they knew each other… until it wasn't.

One day Tink entered the home crying. She fell into the arms of Tyler, going on and on about how her most profitable client had given up on her: That client being a hot-shot mayor of the county and a soon-to-be candidate for Kentucky governorship. A younger man who was quickly climbing the political ladder, was using Tink as a human stress ball, giving her most of the money she would spend on heroin. However as the races finally started to heat up, he decided it best to leave his golden girl. It was a loose end he could not afford in his mind. This left Tink devastated. Once feeling like a princess picked out of poverty was now thrown back into the common, plebeian gutter. Cut off from her source of happiness. This tragedy, of course, all took place on top of a 20-year old mattress, covered in more human fluids and sadness than a handkerchief in the pocket of the world's busiest funeral director.

But her bawling would stop when one the dealers found out she still had enough money for another shot of her medicine. After the initial high, she was soon in a familiar stupor. The other dealers told Tyler if she couldn't pay for another round to just dump her somewhere. Before they left, however, Tink looked deeply into Tyler's eyes and asked him to get more money for her; the man who wronged her would be at a nearby trailer home visiting his grandmother before going off on the campaign trail. And, if nothing else, maybe just a few more minutes with his Bell. Tyler simply looked down at her completely glazed face, planted a kiss on her lips, and left his cowbell at her side. He then stepped out of the home with only an aluminum baseball bat.

Tyler walked seven miles needed to reach the trailer home's location. For the entire walk, Tyler seemed to be in a trance. The way he dragged the bat behind him left a clear trail in the dry dirt road for anyone to follow. But no one was around on this road. It seemed to be clear for this day's walking manifestation of rage and revenge.

Eventually, Tyler reached the park that seemed to match Tink's vague description. He moved through the seemingly abandoned park till he reached the mobile home farthest out from everyone else's. There in the front was a campaign lawn sign of the offending politician. Tyler studied the grinning face on it for a while until his focus was drawn to the mobile home door. There was a sweet-looking old lady who smiled down at the disheveled Tyler. She was none the wiser to Tyler's murderous intent. Hard to be observant when you're partially blind. Instead, she started to talk about how the politician was her grandson and that she was so proud of his progress in the polls. Proud grandma jabber. She would have talked Tyler's ear off for the next hour about the politician's plan to reform schools, a crackdown on drug users, and the promise to return the state to the center of the American spirit if Tyler hadn't cracked her head wide open.

Now while he was by no means a tactician of a superior strategic mind, Tyler had seen enough sketchy drug deals go down to know the meaning of the word bait outside of a fishing context. Not taking mind of the blood trail, he dragged sweet nana's corpse back into the trailer home and waited for his real target.

Through the window blinds after an hour's worth of waiting, he saw a truck seemingly ready to rally a march onto Washington pulled up to the mobile home. It was covered with campaign stickers and posters, all containing the blinding grin of the politician Tyler was set to kill. Soon the man himself stepped out of the truck in boots too nice to have ever been worked in, wearing a button shirt that was exactly the kind Nashville country would eventually kill. All topped off with a grin more plastic than the buttons pinned to his chest. It Seemed Tyler guessed right on what a politician would look like.

This politician in question slowly strode up to the home, calling out for his grammy when he was only a few steps away from the door. He had gone there alone, wanting some quality time with her after being gone for so long at the state capital. He wanted to pay respects to the woman who raised him when his own parents couldn't. When the vacant rocking chair on the small porch finally caught his eye, something deep inside started to sense the off nature of the situation. When he neared the front of the home, the blood trail leading to the door sent him into an immediate panic. Reason would dictate that the last thing one should do is follow a blood trail into a confined space but family wasn't a rational matter for this all too honest man of the people. He quickly rushed to the door, arm stretched out and reaching to fling the door open. Before he could see any more of his grandma's spilled blood, he was subject to the spilling of his own.

Tyler barged through the trailer door, completely catching the politician off balance. He fell to the ground with a dirty thunk, catching a momentary glimpse of Tyler's face before his eyes were thunked into the back of his skull. It was a gruesome scene, involving enough bat swings to kill a bison let alone a pencil-necked politician.

But Tyler would not let up, keeping up the pounding to the face, body, and eventually the truck of the now firmly deceased campaign runner. It was just a whirlwind of rage finally coming out of Tyler. He released every ounce of hatred he had for his father, mother, therapists, dealer bosses, and the entire world all at that moment. His guttural scream was the first thing he vocalized ever since being damned by his mother so long ago in that school. It was one based on the feeling of anger and then release. Release of all that controlled him. For so long he had felt tied to the sins of his family: Always being told what to do by his father, what to believe by his mother, how to feel by the therapists, how to live by the dealers. Him taking that bat to the temples of that old shitbag politician was just about the most freeing thing Tyler could have ever felt. Because it was he who was spilling the blood now, he who was giving out pain, he who was doing things for the one he cared about.

As all of this was finally channeled out, Tyler caught a glimpse of himself in the reflection of the shiny truck door he was smashing. He saw a glimpse of what had become of his face. He rushed to one of the side mirrors to get a clear picture. It was sunken in like he was an understuffed teddy bear. He had a scraggly beard that demanded to be shaved. His eyes were as red as the blood splattered across his face. It was the epitome of a nightmare state of being. But Tyler didn't feel shame at all for his look. One sentence slipped through his dry and cracked lips.

"No one will recognize me..."

With that, he stopped his assault on the truck, looked back down at his previous handy work, and walked off into the open road. Some say he was never caught and just kept walking until he dropped from dehydration. Others claim they saw him as an aimless drifter, still carrying that bat of his. The police claim they shot him down while he was trying to rob a convenience store. Any of these tales simply aren't worth noting down in detail. It changes nothing of what Tyler did. None add clarification to the meaning of all this unholiness. And it's not like it should. Not in my eyes at the very least

Loveless Soulmate

By Alison Paige

I live in a world where everyone has a soulmate.

That used to mean the person you were going to marry, even if you didn't love them. Now we accept that they're merely just your 'other half'. Your soulmate could be your spouse, your best friend, a one-night stand, or someone you'll never see again; they could even be your sibling.

A majority of the world understands that not everyone is going to end up with their soulmate, the two may be connected but that doesn't mean their lives are tied together.

I was never that interested in following the compass on my wrist, I'm aro/ace so I knew I would never be in a relationship with them and it didn't really matter if I became friends with them. My family found it interesting how the girl named after the most romantic flower, didn't experience romantic attraction herself.

There are people whose only goal in life was to find the person fate was pointing them to, who would travel across the world if it meant they *might* find them. I wasn't one of those people, but unfortunately, my soulmate was.

I work as a barista in a café a few miles from where I grew up. Most of the shifts are pretty copy and paste. You have the regulars who always order the same thing at practically the same time every day, the people who insist you messed up their order and wish to speak with the manager, the ones who want to try everything on the menu, and that one person who claims a free drink with their punch card that you know they punched out at home.

It's not always in that order but it's practically guaranteed that one, if not all of them will show up during your shift. We also have our fair share of coffee dates or students coming in to study, but those are hardly as memorable.

I was behind the register taking orders when the door opened; I didn't look up as the bell was hardly anything new.

A man came up to the counter, a big grin on his face. "Can I buy you a drink?" He asked.

"Excuse me?" It wasn't the first time a customer had offered to buy us something from the café, most of the time it was because of the holidays or their way of paying it forward. This man was something else, I had never seen someone this excited to place an order, let alone one that wasn't even for him.

"A drink, I figured I should get you something before I ask you on a date."

He held up his left arm when I gave him a confused look. His compass was red and pointed at me, sure enough when I looked down my own was no longer black and turned towards him.

This man was my soulmate.

I had gone over in my head multiple times what I would say when I ended up meeting them, however my speech would have to wait as a small line started to form behind him.

"Look, my shift ends in half an hour. If you want we can talk after that," I said.

He nodded, "sounds great," a grin still plastered on his face.

I asked him if he wanted anything for himself since he was at the register and punched in his cortado.

"Can I get a name for the order?"

"Chase Frederick."

I didn't need his last name but I didn't comment on it. "That will be out shortly."

I couldn't help but notice how he picked the seat that was the closest to the counter. I had a feeling he wouldn't like being "just friends" but there was nothing I could do about that.

The next thirty minutes passed by painfully slow, my soulmate seated a few feet away as he scrolled through his phone, occasionally glancing in my direction. My coworker Sarah tapped on my shoulder and I moved aside so she could take over the register. I was now free to clock out and have whatever uncomfortable conversation awaited me.

My purse over my shoulder I made my way over to Chase.

"Hey soulmate," he greeted.

I sighed, this wouldn't be an easy conversation. "It's Rose."

I don't know why I introduced myself, I had had a nametag on and I knew he read it. Perhaps I was stalling.

I took a seat across from him, "look Chase, we may be soulmates but there will never be a romantic relationship between us."

It was blunter than I had prepared but those were the words that ended up coming out.

"I'm sure you're great and it would be wonderful if we could be friends. But I'm aromantic, I'll never have type feelings towards you or anyone else that matter," I added.

I wasn't sure what kind of reaction I expected; denial, maybe yelling, but not the one I got.

"Okay."

"Okay?" I didn't think it would be that easy.

"But can I ask you one thing?" He said.

"Sure," I said, I no longer knew where this conversation was headed.

"Can I still take you out on a date? I know you said you don't get those types of feelings but I figure I should still try." He gave a nervous chuckle and I noticed how he kept turning his phone on the table.

I suppose there wouldn't be any harm in one date, he did know this wouldn't lead anywhere after all. "Why not."

We agreed on tomorrow night and exchanged numbers. He waved as he walked out the door, the big smile back on his face.

I couldn't help but wonder what I had gotten myself into.

* * *

"So you finally met them?" asked my cousin Tyler.

I nodded as I hung my coat back in the closet. I wasn't surprised that he had followed me to my room when I told him; Tyler now laid on my bed with his feet against the wall.

"We're getting dinner tomorrow night." Now I had his full attention.

"You're going on a date with him?"

"I guess, technically. He knows I'm aromantic," I said.

"You're going on a date. It doesn't matter if you have a blinking sign, people are oblivious."

I rolled my eyes even though he couldn't see, my back towards him as I grabbed my pajamas. "Well if Chase hasn't gotten it through his head now, he will by the end of the night."

Tyler shrugged as much as he could while laying down. "If you say so, let me know if you need me to fake an emergency tomorrow."

"Thanks but that won't be necessary." At least I sincerely hoped it wouldn't be.

I kicked Tyler out of my room as I left to take a shower and he offered to pick out a movie for us to watch.

I couldn't help but wonder if he was right, did my soulmate really think he'd be able to win me over? I already knew that wouldn't happen. It never would, let alone over one dinner. But some people refuse to understand that, *especially* when it comes to soulmates. I prayed Chase wasn't the same way.

* * *

We had agreed to meet at the local Italian restaurant, already a bit fancier than I hoped. The destination alone made it feel more like a romantic date than two friends getting together. Tyler helped me pick out an outfit, a nice shirt, and a skirt; he said I didn't have to completely dress up but he lovingly refused to let me leave the apartment in jeans.

I couldn't help but stare at my wrist while I waited for Chase to arrive, my leg bouncing on the sidewalk from nerves. I still wasn't used to the red. The arrow moved slightly from side to side. The mark that let everyone know I had met my "other half". Depending on how tonight goes I might get it covered up. There were no rules against getting tattoos over your compass, it was just generally frowned upon.

Chase waved once he came into view and I stood up from the bench to greet him. He wore a fancy dress shirt and nice black pants, thankfully nothing over the top.

"Shall we head in?" I asked.

"We shall." he responded, all smiles

It didn't take too long to get seated, I tried not to immediately look at my menu. I was too antisocial for whatever this "date" was. "Any topics you'd like to discuss?" I said after a minute or two of awkward silence.

"I brought an icebreaker if you'd like to do that," Chase suggested.

"Sounds great."

He pulled a set of notecards out of his pocket, one stack in front of me, one in front of him. He flipped over the first card, a small "1" in the corner, and read the question.

Given the choice of anyone in the world, whom would you want as a dinner guest?

I never thought of that before, there were plenty of famous people I would love to meet but for a whole dinner? I wasn't sure.

I told him my favorite author and he said the president.

Chase gestured for me to flip over the first of my pile. A "2" in the corner of this card; looks like I had the even numbers.

"Would you like to be famous? In what way?" I read.

Chase said he wasn't sure, he had no desire to be at the moment but wanted it to be for helping people if he ever did become famous. I thought being a well-known artist would be nice.

"What kind of art do you like to do?" He asked; this wasn't one of the notecards.

"Digital, but it's more of a hobby." I pulled up my social media when he asked if he could see something. I averaged about a hundred likes per picture, which certainly wasn't horrible, it was more than I ever thought I would get, but it was far from famous.

"These are amazing," Chase said as he scrolled through my page, he left a like on every image he saw.

"Thanks," I tucked a strand of hair behind my ear. Even if the feedback was mostly positive I was always self-conscious when I showed others my work. "Should we continue our icebreaker?"

Another card flipped over. *Before making a telephone call, do you ever rehearse what you are going to say? Why?*

I said it depended on who I was calling: if it was important or work, yes. If it was family or friends I rarely did. He said no.

"How many questions are there?"

"Thirty-six," Chase answered.

I nodded, I knew what he was doing. The thirty-six questions to fall in love. I had heard the first few but never the whole list, I didn't see the point. You couldn't make people love each other with a few questions, or maybe you could, I wouldn't know. I just knew they wouldn't work on me. I didn't say anything about it, I did like the already chosen topics. The waitress stopped by to get our drink orders and I waited to flip over the next card till she was gone.

What would constitute a 'perfect' day for you?

We looked over our menus while we thought about that one, our server would be back soon anyway and as someone who's worked at a restaurant, I always hated when people took forever to decide what they wanted. Chase got the seafood fettuccine alfredo, I chose the chicken pasta in white wine sauce.

"So what would be your *perfect* day?" I asked as I leaned against my elbow.

"I think that would be a nice morning run, followed by a cup of coffee, lunch with my family at my grandparent's diner, and game night with my friends in the evening."

"I don't think I've ever heard someone say they want to start their day with exercise, especially when describing the perfect day," I laughed.

"What about you?"

"Let's see, that would include sleeping in for once, the day off of work. I think I would spend the day at the beach with a good book, and end it with a movie with my cousin Tyler."

Ever since Tyler and I moved in together movie night, practically every night became a sort of tradition.

"What do you consider a 'good book'?" He asked, which wasn't one of the icebreaker questions.

"Mystery, a modern Sherlock Holmes perhaps," I said with a smirk.

He smiled, "I always loved the original stories."

Chase looked down at the table when he realized he had been staring, "question five: *when did you last sing to yourself? To someone else?*"

He started to turn his phone on the table like he did at the café; picking it up onto its side and setting it back down over and over again. Maybe it was something he did when he was nervous or uncomfortable, maybe it was just a fidget. I always played with the spinny ring on my right hand.

"By myself would be the car ride over here, I love singing along to the radio. To someone else that would be with my coworker a few days ago before opening."

Sarah was so excited to show me the latest musical she had found and they were always catchy.

"I also sang to myself today and to someone else that would be at an open mic yesterday," he explained.

"You should let me know when the next one is, I'd love to hear you sing sometime."

Our waitress came back with our food and politely let us know that the plates were hot as she set them down.

"If you want I could sing now," he joked.

I merely laughed and took a bite of food. Thankfully he did so as well so we wouldn't have the entire restaurant's gaze on us. It doesn't matter how good your voice is, people don't start singing in the middle of dinner unless they're paid to.

We set the notecards aside, and both of us agreed to continue the little icebreaker later. Even if they wouldn't make me fall in love, I did enjoy the questions. They were deeper than the standard get to know yous but not so personal that I didn't want to answer.

Over the meal, I learned the basic facts about my soulmate. Chase was twenty-four, two years older than me. He was an apprentice at an electrical company and was taking music lessons from someone he found online. He lived with his best friend and was a Gemini.

I shared the same things about myself if I hadn't already mentioned it: twenty-two, barista, taking graphic design classes, living with my cousin, and Libra.

We liked most of the same things. Same taste in food, and music, we both even preferred TV shows over movies; movies were something I only watched with Tyler.

Chase was easy to like, he was charismatic and awkward, and kind. He was someone I wanted in my life, to learn hobbies with, or even have over for movie night. But as a friend, it would only ever be as a friend.

The bill came and I insisted that we split the check. Chase was the perfect gentleman and opened the door for me, he didn't ask about a second date but technically the night wasn't over.

We walked down a few blocks to a park, we did need to finish those icebreakers after all.

Barely anyone was around as the sun was about to set. I sat down on a swing, my legs slightly pushing me as I rocked back and forth but not enough for them to leave the ground. Chase handed me my stack and followed suit.

It was my turn to read a card, "*If you were able to live to the age of 90 and retain either the mind or body of a 30-year-old for the last 60 years of your life, which would you want?*"

We both agreed on body. While the idea of slowly losing your mind and memories was terrifying, not being able to do anything by yourself for who knows how many years was worse.

"Do you have a secret hunch about how you will die?" He asked. "I think I'll die in a car crash, it's common enough."

"I have a feeling I'll drown in the ocean," I answered.

"That's morbid, I'm surprised you still consider going to the beach a part of your perfect day."

"I'm surprised you still get in a car," I countered.

Name three things you and your partner appear to have in common.

We both liked the color blue, we both preferred underrated characters, and we both liked to sing.

We both never planned to go to college, we both loved animals, and we both had horrible sleep schedules.

For what in your life do you feel most grateful?

I said family, he said life in general, being alive.

If you could change anything about the way you were raised, what would it be?

Chase said he wished he were raised in a Christian household; the difference in religions was a bit of a sore spot in his family. I told him my parents should have gotten divorced sooner, they failed at hiding their constant fights throughout my childhood, they thought they were doing the right thing. But if we had those little changes we might be completely different people today.

Take four minutes and tell your partner your life story in as much detail as possible.

Chase took out his phone and set a timer, I thought for a moment before I hit start.

"When I was little, around eight years old, we went to a family camp a few hours away from here. We got a few hours of free time and we tended to separate from each other as we did our own "age-appropriate" activities. I'd managed to disappear from all the staff members and when I didn't show up for lunch they eventually found me taking a nap in the woods with a baby bunny in my lap. I named him Timmy."

We laughed and joked about the fact that *surprisingly* they wouldn't let me take him home.

I reset the timer for Chase. He shared a story from his freshman year in high school. He and his friends had volunteered to run a haunted house for Halloween and they wanted to make it as scary as possible. They had the standard things like vampires, jump scares, and gory props but they wanted to have something more; for the experience to end with a bang. His current roommate suggested adding some small firecrackers, whatever they could get that was legal. They ended up setting off the fire alarm and got suspended for a week.

"At least I didn't try to burn down my school," I teased.

"It was an accident," he laughed.

If you could wake up tomorrow having gained any one quality or ability, what would it be?

We both went the supernatural route, he chose the power of flight and I said the ability to shapeshift.

I placed the card I had just read at the back of the pile, from what I remembered about the thirty-six questions there were three "parts", and we were now a third through the questions. I wanted to keep going, I liked getting to know him, but I didn't want to give Chase the wrong idea. Was Tyler right? Did he think he had a chance at a romantic relationship even though I told him when we first met that I was aromantic? Did he get false hope with every answer I gave?

He read the next card: *If a crystal ball could tell you the truth about yourself, your life, the future, or anything else, what would you want to know?*

"How I would die, see if my hunch was right." Chase jokingly shook his head at my response. "What about you?" I asked.

"I'd want to know who I'd end up with."

I sighed, *"Is there something that you've dreamed of doing for a long time? Why haven't you done it?"*

If he didn't want to speak to me after tonight, which was understandable, I wanted to enjoy being his friend as long as I could and prayed that I wouldn't lead him on.

We both said we wanted to try skydiving but made no effort to actually do it.

"Maybe that can be the next thing we do together," he said with a smile. At least he didn't say date.

What is the greatest accomplishment in your life?

Mine was when I won an art contest a year or two ago; his was being the person he wanted to be. Chase explained how he used to put everyone else's needs and wants before his, which isn't necessarily a bad thing, but what he did wasn't healthy. It took him a few years to finally work on his mental health.

I smiled. I knew that wasn't the easiest thing to do, but we both knew now wasn't the right time for that deep of a conversation. We continued, answering a little quicker as it got late.

What do you value most in a friendship?

We both said loyalty and trust.

What is your most treasured memory?

Mine was some Christmas from when I was little, there was nothing special about it but it was something I loved to think back on. All of us were in matching pajamas while we sat around the tree with a pile of presents. Some holiday movie on in the background and gingerbread cookies in the oven, they tasted like cardboard but we still ate the whole batch.

Chase said his was when his adoptive sister Kathrin asked him to be her son's godfather. His nephew/godson Jonny was three years old.

What is your most terrible memory?

That one got brushed over with vague answers. It didn't matter if we were supposed to honestly answer them all, "icebreaker" or not, we weren't ready to discuss that one yet.

If you knew that in one year you would die suddenly, would you change anything about the way you are now living? Why?

I said I would do all the things I was afraid to do; I would quit my job and live off my savings, and make the most of my borrowed time. He told me something similar, how he would treat every day as if it were his last and do his best to have no regrets.

"What does friendship mean to you?" I read. We were twenty questions in, the stars now visible in the dark, slightly cloudy sky.

Chase said it was one of the things that made life worth living, I said it was everything.

We moved to the playground and sat across from each other on the plastic, hole-filled floor. I pointed out Orion and a few other constellations that were noticeable. I couldn't help but smile when he recited the Greek myth of Orion and shared the jokes his grandpa would make about Ursa Minor.

Card number twenty-two was flipped over, Chase forgot to write down number twenty-one so we moved on. *Alternate sharing something you consider a positive characteristic of your partner. Share a total of five items.*

"Kind," he started.

"Funny."

"Thoughtful."

"Optimistic."

"Artistic."

"Friendly," I said with a smile.

"Intelligent," he replied.

"Considerate."

"Likable."

"Adventurous," I finished.

Chase grinned and flipped over the next question: *How close and warm is your family? Do you feel your childhood was happier than most other people's?*

Despite my mom and dad slightly hating each other, they were good parents. Minus their fights I think I had a good, happy childhood.

Chase said his family was very close, he and all of his siblings were adopted. He said he wouldn't change that for the world.

How do you feel about your relationship with your mother?

We both said that we could be closer but it was good.

We were now in the third set of questions. They were more detailed and more personal: *If you were going to become a close friend with your partner, please share what would be important for him or her to know.*

I re-shared that I was aromantic. Part of me was nervous that he would want to end the night there. He merely smiled and shared that his job didn't give him a lot of free time. I hoped that was a good sign.

Tell your partner what you like about them; be very honest this time, saying things that you might not say to someone you've just met.

I liked how sweet and carefree he was. From our rushed and unexpected meeting to this moment he had shown me nothing but kindness. Even when I could tell he wasn't sure what to say it was never uncomfortable. I told him I really hoped we could be close friends after this.

He liked that I was real, that I was kind and honest. That I didn't push him away from the start, that I gave him a chance. He said he also hoped we could be close friends.

The next one was more lighthearted: *Share with your partner an embarrassing moment in your life.* We shared silly school stories and laughed at each other's humiliating stories.

I read number thirty which was similar to one we already had: *When did you last cry in front of another person? By yourself?* Neither of us remembered when that was, each I suppose is a good thing as that means we haven't cried recently.

Someone came by and asked if we could leave the park, it was already 11:00 PM so this area was technically closed. We apologized and quickly left. Chase read the next card as we walked to our cars. *Tell your partner something that you like about them.*

"Didn't we just answer that a few questions ago?" I asked.

"I think we did," he laughed and gestured for me to flip over number thirty-two.

What, if anything, is too serious to be joked about?

We both agreed on suicide and other similar topics.

If you were to die this evening with no opportunity to communicate with anyone, what would you most regret not having told someone? Why haven't you told them yet?

I wasn't sure, I'd like to think that I tell people everything important. Chase said we can circle back to that one as he also wasn't sure.

Your house, containing everything you own, catches fire. After saving your loved ones and pets, you have time to safely make a final dash to save any one item. What would it be? Why?

"Probably a box of things I consider irreplaceable, you?"

"My computer," I answered.

"Your computer?" He said with a small laugh.

"Hey, I paid a lot for that thing."

Our vehicles were in sight and we had two questions left, this would be the end of our late night.

Of all the people in your family, whose death would you find most disturbing? Why?

"My cousin Tyler, I've known him my whole life and live with him. I don't want to think about him dying anytime soon."

Chase nodded and said his father; he had been there for him for as long as he could remember, he couldn't imagine what it would be like without him.

I flipped over my last notecard, the last of these thirty-six "icebreaker" questions.

Share a personal problem and ask your partner's advice on how he or she might handle it. Also, ask your partner to reflect back to you on how you seem to be feeling about the problem you have chosen.

Maybe it was because we wanted something to come back to, maybe it was because we didn't want to ask the other for help. Whatever the reason was, we didn't answer the last of the questions to fall in love.

Chase kissed my cheek and wished me good night. I smiled and waved farewell as I got in my car. That was the end of our "date".

* * *

I didn't hear from Chase the next day or the day after that. It hurt but I wasn't sure if I should say something; if he didn't want to be friends I didn't want to push it. Tyler said there was no harm in sending a simple "hello" but I felt like if I sent something I should say more. I wasn't sure why but that's how I felt.

I was near the end of my shift at the café, Sarah was in the back making the drinks while I punched them in as normal. The bell rang; I didn't look up from my task, the bell rings all the time.

"How can I help you?" I asked.

Chase stood on the other side of the counter, "A cortado and a conversation if you're free," he said with a shy smile.

I typed it in. "I get off in fifteen," so similar to the day we met.

He paid for his drink and sat down at the same spot as before. I didn't know what to expect from this conversation but I tried to stay hopeful.

"Rose," Sarah said as she tapped my shoulder.

"Hm?"

"Is that your soulmate?" She asked with a small gesture towards Chase.

I nodded and took the next person's order.

It was time to clock out when she spoke again. "I don't mean to pry, but is he also aromantic?"

I hung my apron up with a sigh, "no." I didn't see her reaction and made my way over to Chase. "Can I sit here?"

"Of course."

I took the seat across from him. "I'm sorry I didn't message you," he said.

"You don't have to apologize."

He shook his head, "it took me too long to accept that I wouldn't marry my soulmate, you told me from the start that wouldn't happen."

I looked away, so that is why he didn't reach out; because I would never love him that way. Chase continued to speak, "I thought maybe it would be different since I was your soulmate, I was even foolish enough to try those 'scientifically proven' questions to fall in love."

"I knew what they were from the start," I said. He seemed surprised by my answer. "I'm sorry if I lead you on by wanting to continue the questions, but I liked getting to know you and I didn't want that to stop."

There was a moment of silence, a moment too long in my opinion.

"Friends?" He asked.

I smiled, "I would like that." Part of me couldn't help but feel relieved. My soulmate and I were on the same page, we were honest with each other, we were friends.

I got a drink of my own and we stayed at the café; we conversed and laughed. Sort of like part two of last night, but this wasn't a date. There were no questions to fall in love, there was no lying about who we were to get the other to like us. Just two friends hanging out. It was wonderful.

"You know, if you want to be in a relationship I know someone I could set you up with," I offered.

"Really, who?"

I smiled and gestured towards the counter, my coworker Sarah at the register.

"What about her soulmate?" Chase asked, her red compass visible from here with her short sleeves.

"He has a boyfriend so there shouldn't be any problems there," I answered.

I had a feeling they would get along, and the two of them looked like they would be a cute couple.

We continued our conversation while Chase debated if he should go talk to her, which I eventually convinced him to. And I was right, the two of them hit it off almost immediately.

Our relationship may not have started how either of us expected but no matter what happened, I'm glad my other half is a part of my life.

Six Feet Under One Mile

by Ariana Dobrostal

She was there because she could burn the world between her fingers. I was there because I was a hero.

I'd never call myself a hero. No real hero would, right? But it's not that I wouldn't do it because I was so virtuous that even the slightest diversion from the right path would physically pain me nor so humble I couldn't utter one word of praise on my behalf. No, I was none of these things.

What separated me from a hero was the lack of the core hero ingredient: good intentions.

I didn't feel bad for not being a hero. Not many people truly were. I'm fairly sure admitting you're no hero brings you closer to being one than trying to mask yourself with obnoxious displays of fake goodness. I knew many people like that in my village. They carried groceries for old people and donated bread to the orphanage, but once the real problem presented itself, they presented only cowardice and passivity.

Then from the shadows emerged an unlikely hero: Nacai Nonem, a no-name farmer with nothing to lose and no one to lose him. I was the perfect candidate for this mission: alone and worthless, belonging to the shadows. So, to the shadows, I went.

I went on a search for the wish-granting monster at the end of the cave. Tale as old as time, yet there wasn't one person in my village that didn't believe in it wholeheartedly. The challenge was simple: you enter the cave, find the monster at its end, and make a wish. Then you had to climb uphill back to civilization.

Once you stepped your foot outside the cave, your wish was fulfilled. Just like that. Anything in the world could be yours. You had only one wish, but it could be anything at all. Yet, as long as people lived comfortably, they didn't reach into darkness for gold. No one dared to risk their lives to reach their dreams. It's only in times of need we reach for miracles.

"How deep do you think it is?" Izzy asked.

Her name was read as "Easy", but nothing was easy with her. She was the only fire witch left, orphaned since birth and in great debt to the village. She was the opposite of me in both looks and demeanor: fair, cheerful, and bright. The real hero, the fire to my shadow, and the pain in my ass.

"How could I know?" I said.

"I didn't ask how deep it really is, just how deep you think it is."

"Your guess is as good as mine," I said. "I'm not a huge fan of wild guessing."

"Come on, you have nothing to lose. By the end of this, we'll either die or become best friends."

"Or remain perfect strangers."

She went silent, but I felt her unhappy stare at the back of my neck. I sighed, "I'd say around half a mile deep."

"Only half?" She sounded even more disappointed than when I ignored her.

"The deepest cave in the world is only around one mile deep."

I heard her steps grow faster and in a second, she was in front of me, light melting on her face. With the light coming directly from below at such intensity, she looked sinister, her eyes impossibly big and her teeth impossibly bright. She smiled widely like she knew exactly how to make a grown man weep.

"Why do you assume we're not in the deepest cave right now?"

With that, she turned on her heel and skipped ahead, forcing me to follow her shadow.

She was like a little pixie of the cavern, jumping from stalagmite to stalactite and making shadows dance on the walls, hunting you till you fall and haunting you when you sleep. I sped up just enough not to lose her, although it was hard to lose the fire in the dark, no matter how fast it flew. I enjoyed some time alone, even if she was just around the corner.

With a moment to think, I realized I wasn't the biggest fan of caves. The terrain was pointy and damp, making me slip and stumble. It was the most uncomfortable slide in the world, slowly angled and high in friction. Even higher in humidity, dripping drop by drop and missing the value of water that carves its paths.

At least I had to admit that minerals created interesting shadows. If I was still a child, I'd be able to see shapes in it: a huge octopus stretching its tentacles or a tree losing leaves, or maybe a queen living in a different universe even if we breathe the same air. Or even a hero, helping me save the world.

Only, I was a kid a long time ago and couldn't keep him, so I saw only rock icicles that could fall on me and spikes I could fall onto. I heard Izzy gawking at a statue of a 'sleeping kitten' and felt relieved. At least one of us was able to keep their spirit, if not their sanity.

We walked down the same trail for what felt like an eternity. There were no splitting paths, no sudden changes in sound or scenery, just the same drops and sharp rocks surrounding one dull straight line. Izzy didn't try to talk to me again, and enough time passed that I began to question whether I liked it or not.

But nothing could last forever, so at one point the light stopped escaping me. It waited, like the light at the end of the tunnel, only it wasn't nearly the end. It was a slightly wider area, not bigger than my old cottage, but in comparison to a narrow track, it seemed enormous.

The number of minerals dwindled, leaving the room bare except for a flowstone centerpiece. Izzy sat right under it, letting each droplet fall on her forehead before it evaporates from her warmth. Her palms were hidden under two vibrant flames that did wonders to the glossy surface.

"Took you long enough," she laughed. "I think this is a fine place for a camp, don't you?"

I shook my head. "We have to keep moving."

"You say that, and yet you can't keep up with me," she said. She giggled when I frowned. "Oh, come on, don't be like that. Sit with me. We can eat something, chat a bit. Do you hate fun?"

"Maybe," I sighed. "Alright, we'll take a break."

I sat next to her and opened our tiny supply of dried meat and bread. It might be the last one we'll have, but the people left in the village had their last meals yesterday.

"Do you think it's real? The wish-granting monster?" she asked between bites. She stared at me with anticipation, checking if I didn't speak because of a full mouth. When she realized I didn't, she continued, "Dumb question, of course. I know you don't. You probably just did this because of boredom. Or spite. Or both."

"I do," I said. "I do believe it's real."

She smiled. "So, you do? Why?"

"Because there has to be some hope left in the world."

Izzy chuckled. "That doesn't count. You can't believe in something because of some pessimistic quote, it's contradictory."

"Why do you believe then?" I asked.

"Who said I did?"

"I know you do. The village knows you do. The whole world knows you do."

She shook her head. "I'm not sure I do. That's why I'm here – to find out."

My jaw dropped. Izzy wasn't as naïve as she seemed. Maybe no orphan was allowed to be.

"What would you do if it's not?" I had to know. I didn't know what'd I do if it was not real.

She took a long pause then grinned. "Then I'll become one."

I got my hopes up too high. I nodded to her with the notion that our conversation came to a close. I turned my back to her, and we crumpled on the floor next to each other, drifting to very different but equally dangerous dreams.

The reality was even more dangerous. One scream and I was wide awake, on my feet before my mind caught my body in a nerve net. Izzy was on the floor, struggling as a monster held her down. There were flicks of fire between periods of darkness when she attacked, but I couldn't distinguish what an intruder was. Its shape wasn't familiar.

Nonetheless, I jumped it, pushing it off her. Its skin was smooth as glass, cold as it too. I shivered as I regained my balance, but the monster had already hidden from me. Izzy jumped on her feet, propelling flames left and right. Fireballs were more intense but shorter than her usual flames. I saw sudden fragments of motion, flashes of the cave rotating around me.

"Please stop, we can talk, please," I mustered in all the languages I knew. I squeezed my mind till it was dry. Nothing. It occurred to me too late that it might not have a language at all. I noticed it approaching me too late too.

The monster climbed up the walls as easily as we walked down the dusty streets. It glided over the flowstone, as if it was on ice.

I saw it more clearly as it lunged toward me, its antennas and shells moving in sync. It was an oblong bug, with translucent skin and millions of legs, some starting on its belly, not only on the sides. It was a bug the size of a sheep. All its organs wobbled inside it, held together only by the jelly of its flesh.

Izzy summoned the whole underworld. I had to close my eyes to keep them. Blinding light could burn the whole underground and she didn't care if we were sealed here forever, as long as the creature evaporated into thin air. Each of her fingertips burst a flame that turned into a fireball, flying steadily to its target. Only, it was a moving target.

I found myself on the floor with my vision blurry. My arm stung, my eye twitched and I felt the strong smell of burnt corpses. I wasn't one of them, but that was enough to calm the buzzing in my mind. I heard all languages screaming in me, cursing me in a union, then priceless silence.

"Are you alive?" I heard Izzy ask. She didn't seem concerned, maybe because she believed in me, maybe because she didn't care.

"What happened?" I asked, trying to sit up. My eyes wandered, looking for the monster, but found something much more disturbing. My right arm was in shambles, the whole forearm burnt to the point of resembling cave walls. Seeing my own flesh that rugged and coarse made it hurt more and I fell back, breathing heavily.

"Nacai!" Now she did sound worried. She kneeled beside me and brought water to my mouth. "Drink. Breathe. I'm so sorry."

I let the fresh water clean my throat, feeling I could drown it in with no regrets. Then I remembered we didn't have fresh water. Or any, for that matter.

I spit it out immediately, my sweet heaven becoming hell by the second. "What is that?"

"Monster water," she said casually.

"Monster water?" I wiped my lips in disgust. "You made me drink from the monster's corpse? First, you curse me with fire, then with water."

"I drank it myself," she said defensively. "It's good. Better than the water we have left anyway."

I remembered the water we had when we left – a bottle half empty. For some, it might have been half full, but I was positive no one would call it that by the time of the attack. Izzy saved my life and our water supply in one fell swoop.

"Sorry," I said. "Thank you for saving me."

She smiled. "Now we're talking. I'm glad I saved you for that sentence alone."

We put our camp back into the backpack and moved on. Even with my wound, we couldn't rest one bit, I was painfully aware of it now. Every second crushed our odds, and they looked grim in the beginning. I wrapped my arm into a spare shirt, not the best solution, but not the worst either. I tried to block the pain by counting my steps.

The cave became more twisty, making it hard to navigate. Each tunnel split into many more. With every choice to commit to a certain tunnel, we took another risk, pilling up into infinity. Izzy brushed it off, saying that all roads lead to the same destination, but her voice didn't sound right. She marked each entrance we walked through with a burned handprint, holding her hand patiently on freezing walls till she melted them.

The deeper we went, the less Izzy spoke. Even though we didn't encounter any more direct dangers, her spirit was broken. She was a wingless pixie, moping beside me. She didn't deserve to be like that. There was a price for saving my life and I was going to pay it.

"Were you afraid?" I asked gently. She jumped in surprise at my voice. "Of the monster?"

"So, you don't want our every bonding moment to be by the campfire after all," she laughed.

"Just answer the question," I said.

"Not really," she said. "When you control something that can leave thousands without a home, you are rarely afraid."

I nodded. "Thought so."

"Oh, actually, this is interesting," she said, her spirits climbing. She opened her arms and her flames stretched, looking like a ribbon between her palms. "Want to hear a story?"

"Make it a good one."

"Wait!" She grabbed me by my left arm. "You need to pay close attention to this."

She opened her palms towards me like she was giving something to me. At first, all I could see were flames – magical and majestic and mesmerizing – but nothing new. Then it happened: the first ripple and then the other and another. The fire was alive. It infused with life before my very eyes.

"When I was little, I was always afraid," Izzy started. The fire recast into a little girl in a simple style, but wild in motion. She ran along her palm, making backflips and cartwheels. "I was left alone. I never knew of security. Families in the village gave me a changing home. I was passed around like a doll everyone liked, but no one liked enough."

The fire girl stumbled and fell, the cheerfulness from before exorcized. Her body started skipping again, but she didn't control it anymore. Her small frame moved from side to side against her will, violently. Then subtly, her shape lost its roundness, becoming rougher. It was barely noticeable, but I noticed, and couldn't notice anything else. Only her pointy features that once were smooth.

"I constantly felt the unease," she said. "What if they abandon me? I knew only our village. Only they could protect me, but who'd protect me from them? Kids picked fights with me daily. I was an easy target, always polite and sweet, always doing everything so they like me, so they keep me for another day."

The fire girl stood perfectly still.

"One day, I was playing with a group of girls my age at the park. I was six. One of them brought a new doll and we took turns carrying it. When it was my turn, she wouldn't let me take it. She said that if my mom didn't hold me, then I shouldn't hold a baby either."

I frowned. I knew where this story was going. It started for me when I was six too.

"I got so mad," she said shakily, "that I felt my face burning. The flame lit up inside me – and it stayed. I reached out for the doll and the doll went up in flames."

The fire girl did as well, her hair becoming the flame that consumed her. Fire killed by fire.

"After that, they behaved perfectly around me. After that, I didn't hear as much as one bad word directed at me. After that," she smiled, "I wasn't afraid."

She brought her palms together, signaling the end of the show, and created a normal flame in its place. I felt a sudden sting as it ended but was grateful I witnessed it. "It was beautiful."

"Thank you," Izzy smiled. "You're getting better by the minute. What happened? I hit your head as well?"

After she shared such a thing with me, I wanted to share something as well. My chest felt hollow. I never thought I'd share my secrets with anyone, but I also never thought I'd end up in a cave with a chatterbox I didn't hate. After all, once it's over, we'd never see each other again.

"Want to hear a story too?" I asked and her eyes lit up. "Mine won't be as long. Actually, it might be very short. But here it goes: when I was little, I played in a barn a lot. My father had a cow and having a cow was even rarer back then than it is now. I spent so much time with her, that I started talking to her. And, after some time, she started talking to me. At first, I thought I was crazy. Then I tested it on multiple animals and travelers from far-off places and... I'm not crazy," I said. "I'm a witch."

Her eyes displayed no surprise, no shock, no wonder. They stayed positively happy, but not impressed. I never thought my biggest secret would cause such a weak reaction.

"I know," she shrugged.

"You do?" I was surprised enough for both of us.

"Yeah, every witch can feel other witches," she said. "Can't you?"

I blinked in surprise, trying to feel Izzy's magical energy, but only feeling the thermal energy she always radiated, the warmth intertwined with the very core of her being.

"No, I'm totally messing with you," she grinned. "I just heard you screaming nonsense at the top of your lungs, and you don't seem like the type of guy to scream nonsense, so I assumed they were magic spells."

I sighed. "They were no spells, they were desperate pleas to the monster."

"I know that now," she said. "I know everything now. Except..."

I knew it. She was going to ask me to talk in animal languages and make a fool of myself. I braced myself for the weirdest animals I could think of, deciding on a whim that I'd give her one if she chose it wisely.

"What would you wish for if you had a choice?" She didn't choose it wisely.

"What do you mean?" I feigned surprise.

"If you didn't have to save the village, what would you ask the wish-granting monster for?"

She was still smiling, but her posture got serious, more wooden. Like she turned into a doll. "Be careful with it. It can be anything in the world, so if you choose wrong, you'll regret it forever."

"To start my life anew in a big town, to be rich and happy," I said readily. "It's what I'd wish for."

It's not what I'd wish for. It's what I will wish for.

"That was fast," she laughed. "Did you think about it a lot?"

"As much as any other person who heard the story," I said. "But it doesn't matter now. Now it's different."

We arrived at another crossroad, this one consisting of only two tunnels. As she was marking the right entrance, I asked, "What would you wish for?"

She took a moment to think, then said more confidently than me, "Even if the village wasn't in danger, I'd still wish for it to prosper."

She finished the mark and turned to me. "Even if it isn't perfect, it's the only place I know. The place I love."

I nodded. "It's admirable, to be that selfless."

She shook her head. "It's not. It's as selfish as your wish is, even more so. But it seems innocent."

We walked in silence some more, with a new skill of mutual understanding. It was as if the rock fell off my chest. Maybe there was some merit in sharing your secrets and desires with other people. Maybe I only needed one language.

With silence, the pain returned. I managed to dig it under countless layers of distractions and words, but now it emerged on the surface, pushing me to the ground. The cloth I wrapped around it got damped from the liquid air, making it less painful, but felt more like a walking infection.

"Izzy, I need to rest," I said. "My arm is getting worse. I need to inspect it."

Izzy grabbed my other arm, ignoring my request. "Quiet."

The silence was the opposite of what I needed. I needed something to save me from the pain, not push me into it.

"Can you hear it?" she smiled. "Tell me you hear it."

"Hear what?" I heard other words, words in languages I didn't like.

"Water!" she exclaimed. "There is water near."

"So?" My mind was a blank slate, my flesh a stained one.

"It means we're near the end," she beamed. "The water digging the cave, it has to end up somewhere. It will end up in the end, right? We're near the end!"

I smiled. Through the agony, a silver lining found me and dragged me along. Even if my only wish at the time was to go home – to any home – I found the strength to keep moving.

We picked up the pace. I got dizzy as Izzy ran forward, always one step ahead. The ground became wetter. Our hopes became stronger. We were so close we could feel it, on our skin, in our ears, in our nose. Soon we'd see it too, see the great monster everyone knew about, but no one knew.

Izzy tripped on a puddle and fell, but the only thing she did was laugh. She splashed it around like a crazy person. For a fire witch, she really enjoyed the water.

"How long have we been down here? Hours, days?"

I smiled. "How could I know?"

After a few minutes, we were knees deep in water, rippling the floor with every step. My arm got huge, swollen like a soaked sponge. I felt the pain grow along with its source. But if I gave up now, I'd forever be that person who died a step before the finishing line.

"I can see it!" Izzy screamed. She sent more flames to the front, helping me see it too.

The wish-granting monster at the end of the cave turned out to be the wish-granting cave at the end of itself. The fully formed face stood in the wall, smiling blissfully. It was the last wall, the wall at the end. It closed the cave.

The face was pointy like the rest of it, Izzy's shadows making it even sharper. Big eyebrows and pronounced cheekbones, eyes closed, but lips slightly parted. It would speak any moment. The cave's lips opened slowly, like they wanted to chew on me. Izzy was speechless and I couldn't allow myself to be.

"Are you the wish-granting cave?" I tried the language I grew to like, but to no avail.

The face froze for a long moment before it proceeded to move. The water beneath it shifted like it was meant to run through its veins, lending it life. Waves splashed our legs, pushing us away and pulling us in. The face struggled to move, the rocks twitching unnaturally. Not that there were many natural things about the living cave that granted wishes.

Finally, something clicked and it was ready to start anew after long years of being forgotten. It picked up the pace and roared into our faces, blowing our hair like a wind. The sound it produced was menacing, mocking even, and I couldn't understand it.

I brushed away all my fears and focused on sounds alone. Howling blocked my ears, sending shivers down my spine, but I listened. I caught every whisper, every gasp of air, hoping for real words to leave its mouth.

When they did, I wasn't ready for them. "What do you wish for?"

My throat was impossibly sore. I translated my selfish wish into the ancient language I never heard before as easily as breathing but found talking hard. I breathed in and out, concentrating on the spot on the floor and hoping that the cave would be as patient with me as I was with it.

The flames weren't as patient. Izzy put the fire out as suddenly as kids blew candles off their birthday cake. One second you saw it and the next you drowned in the darkness. My light left me in shadows.

"Make the right choice," she said in a cold voice, "and I'll light it up again."

The air was freezing. Izzy was boiling. My arm devoured me. The floor was wet and my mouth was dry.

I licked my lips and turned silence into sound.

Half of Me

By Shannon Yukumi

It was a brisk winter morning by the lake the last time I met the demon.

He appeared as he always did: unexpected but with the subtle, foreboding twinge of cold twisting my stomach. Shivering, I pulled the heavy *uwagi* coat tighter over my kimono--the demon offered his Montbell down jacket. I declined.

Following the creaking bamboo grove on my left and keeping the demon between myself and the reflections of the orange sunrise over the lake to my right, we shuffled along the marked trail, our breath misting the air and mingling between us. With falling snow coating our tracks behind us, we walked a good hour in silence before his graveled voice carved through it.

"Do you still hate Japan, Naomi?"

Fear didn't grip me. Instead, my chest tightened with nervousness, my throat with shyness. I kept moving forward, one foot in this world and the other in the next. Snow danced in a breeze, powdering the slumbering pines, barren cherry and plum trees, and my wrinkled face, which began to match the paleness of the demon's own.

Folding his arms, he again broke our silence. "Japan has insulated coats, you know." He frowned. "You'll freeze out here in a kimono."

"I'm fine." I rubbed my hands together. Paper-thin and dappled with dark liver spots contrasting with my slightly lighter brown skin, they were numb to the cold. "I brought something to warm me up."

The demon sniffed; a sly smile parted his lips just enough to see one scraggly fang. "That's why I came."

"That's why you always come."

"Tell me again why you let me."

"You help me understand things."

"Is something troubling you?"

In a sense. But I wasn't ready to let him know that. Instead, I unwrapped a red *furoshiki* cloth and handed him something I had kept out of my world for so long: a piece of cornbread.

He snatched it and scarfed it down. "I haven't had this in years."

"Brings back memories, doesn't it?"

"I wish they sold these here."

"I'm baking it again because I finally understand what I am."

"Took you long enough."

"Do you remember how many times you tried to tell me?"

"I can't quite recall." His quiet smile said differently.

I bowed my head, clutching the *furoshiki* to my chest like armor. "Three times."

"Do tell."

As snow gathered upon his hair of matted snakes, he listened to my memories float in the breath connecting us, the lake's rolling waves lapping away my words.

First meeting:

In the schoolyard

"Hey, Naomi. Hey! Wait up," the demon said, his high-pitched nasally voice needling into my ears. He sidled up to me, sniffing the hardened leather *randoseru* on my back like a stray dog. "Got any left? Gimme some."

The demon liked cornbread. Throwing him a piece usually got rid of him. Rummaging through the cloth pouch hanging off my side to pick through the lunch I wasn't planning on eating anyway, I averted my eyes so I wouldn't have to look at the wriggling mass of worms piled atop his head and his inward-turning fangs. But mostly, to avoid looking into his fiery eyes or seeing his dark skin.

"Give it over, Naomi."

I fumbled out the entire cut of bread and handed it to him. Our hands brushed as he took it; the two tones of our skin briefly matched shades: chocolate-brown against a light bronze. The sun had shaded his, unlike mine, which had been dark since I was born. *He* could be as pale as a lily if he wanted to, but spending so much time out of the world he should have stayed in had tanned it.

My teeth ground together at the thought.

"Where do you get this bread anyway?"

"My mom makes it." I bowed my head and swiftly jogged toward the iron gate of the school.

Catching my sleeve, he forced me to face him. Crumbs dappled his shirt as he gobbled down the last of the bread. "Why're you leaving?"

Frustration pierced my throat hard enough to shove an answer through my clenched jaw: "Because I hate Japan."

"But you've never lived anywhere else."

"That's exactly it!" I bolted.

Reaching the front gate, I jerked it open just enough to slip through. Now I was free of stares, sniggers, classmates' nagging to stroke my curly hair, their giggles when I struggled with words and insistence that I wasn't one of them. Even though I was--sort of. My father is Japanese.

Well, they wouldn't "other" me anymore. Especially not Yui and her horrible group. For the rest of today at least.

Though the demon shouldn't have been able to leave the school grounds, he wiggled his way through the gate, grinning. Cornbread mash filled the gaps in his teeth. "Yui again?"

"Leave me alone."

Skipping ahead of me, he delighted in getting in my way and making my steps falter. "They get to you 'cause you let 'em, you know."

"I don't let them. They attack me."

"You're putting a target on yourself." He pointed to the woven Shinto *omamori*--talisman--hanging off my *randoseru* and then to the golden cross around my neck. "Two targets, really."

"Three if you count my skin." I buttoned up my top button to hide my mother's birthday gift.

"If you hide that you'll get teased more."

"It doesn't matter. I can't hide my skin."

The demon snort-laughed. "You *could*, you know, like a mummy."

"How do you ignore them? The stares and the name-calling, I mean."

The demon shrugged, his pointed shoulders bending skyward like two orange traffic cones. "I guess they don't bother me as much as they do you. The others don't see me as I am because I don't let them. That's all."

"Maybe they're blind," I said. "Or you are."

"I am, now!" He shut his eyes tight and stuck his arms straight out, shifting from foot to foot as he shuffled around me. Pointed nails on the end of his fingers swiped playfully at the air.

I turned and ran. He gave chase. Then I chased him. Then we chased dragonflies until we both collapsed from exhaustion beneath a huge stone *torii* gate leading to a shrine to *Omi Hachiman*--whoever that was.

Sweating, he sucked on my thermos while I caught my breath. Above me, a thick twisting rope--*shimenawa*--dangled between the gate's stone columns, and hanging off it, four strings of zig-zagging folded paper--*shide*--swayed in a breeze. Made of a strip of paper folded into several uniform rectangles that looked stuck together at the corners, the *shide* had a curious quadruple Z-shape. The rectangles seemed to fight against each other as the wind lifted the paper at the angles, but they didn't tear away.

"Praise and lies may be snakes and spies so find the clear path between them."

I cocked my head at the demon. "What?"

"You asked how I ignore bullies. That's what my dad tells me to do."

Advice from Enma, the King of Hell, himself. "Does it help?"

"Sometimes." He handed my thermos back. "But it's easier if I just focus on me, you know?"

I didn't know, and his smirk told me he knew I didn't.

"Nao, you're so hung up on what you are, you can't see who you are. But we're sixth-graders now. Almost adults. We can't hide what we are, not to ourselves or others, so just be what you are and find who you are."

"I know what I am!"

"Tell me."

"Yamamura Naomi."

"Keep going."

"I dunno. I like butterflies and the color orange."

The demon laughed. "You're not saying it. It was hard for me to say 'it,' too. We're different, you and me. You gotta see that. My dad told me I had a truth I couldn't embrace, and everything got better when I could. I mean, when I could embrace my truth, the difference between *me* and *them*, then people saw me for me."

"What does that mean?"

"Embrace? It's like a hug. You gotta give the thing you hate the most a big ol' hug. Or you know, you'll always be sad or angry or something."

What kind of demon was he, anyway? Hug the things you hate?

"Who do you hate right now," he asked.

"Yui." And there was no way I was going to give her a hug.

"Why?"

"She makes fun of me. Calls me 'burnt girl' and 'dirty.'"

"Because of your skin."

I nodded.

"Do you hate your skin?"

I nodded harder. "If I had skin color like everyone else--"

"You don't. And who gave you your skin?"

"My mother. She's not Japanese."

"Do you hate her?"

I folded my arms. It was *her* fault I was who I was.

But hate? *Hate?* Bunching the fabric of my collar, I clutched the golden cross I had hidden.

Mother knew me as well as she knew the color of her own skin--black, and two shades darker than mine. Her skin drew her away from America. She wanted to live in a world where she would have a clearly defined reason to be an outsider, not just because of her skin. She chose Japan and struggled with its language, culture, and ideals. But her struggles made her stronger. She said it would make me stronger, too.

I doubted that.

The demon frowned. "Do you, Nao? Do you hate her? You gotta say it if you do."

I toed the gravel underneath my feet. Whenever I had a problem, her smile was a warm tea on a cold morning, and her hugs tight. "I can't hate my mother." She gave three gifts to me, after all. Life. A cross, though Father didn't believe. And her skin. "I don't."

"Then you can't hate yourself. Because that would be like hating your mom."

"Did your father say that, too?"

The demon's grin became fire. "Yup. If you can't hug your skin, go hug your mother. I do. I give my dad loads of hugs."

I smirked at his casual admission of affection, but he just grinned harder.

"Embrace your truth, Nao."

"They'll still make fun of me."

"They still make fun of me. Because being different in Japan is like being a wolf in a flock of sheep. Except the sheep eat you." He gnashed his teeth and growled. Cornbread bits spotted the *torii* gate. "We are strong wolves, though, right? We can't let the sheep see that, or they'll get scared off. I don't want to be scary. There's nothing wrong with wolves living with sheep, you know."

"What if I want to be a sheep?"

"You can wear their wool if you want, but you'll look silly."

"Are you saying, 'just be myself?'" I wrinkled my nose at him. "Being yourself" didn't work here. Japan wasn't an American after-school special.

His eyes darkened as though insulted, but he just laughed. "No. That's stupid." He squinted his eyes up at the crooked paper *shide* above us. "If those paper things there were straight, they'd be boring, huh? But they're not. They're cool. They know they have to zig and zag, or people wouldn't think they're cool. And what if they were straight?"

"But they can't be straight. *Shide* aren't made that way."

"Right. And if they were, people would yell and scream to change them back. So why try changing what they are?" He stood and stretched. "Being crooked is cool. And if you try to fix yourself, people will see right through it. Got it? My dad says, 'Don't worry about being yourself.' You will be, even if you try not to be. People make fun of you if you try not to be you, right? But if you be what you are, that won't matter. First, you gotta know what you are."

"Your dad is pretty smart."

"He sure is. So you gotta know who you are. So who are you?"

"Naomi."

"And what are you?"

I wrung my hands. "Half. Half-Japanese. *Hāfu*." I slurred out the English loanword with the thickest accent I could muster.

The demon's brows furrowed. "*No*, you're *not*. You're not half of *anything* because your mother wasn't born here. You are Japanese. Like me."

"But--"

"The *shide* is Japanese because of the way it's folded. But it's still just paper." He shoved a pointed finger into my chest, striking my cross and making it dig into my skin. "You. Are. Japanese. A bit crooked, but that makes you cool, Nao."

He ran off, leaving me under the *torii*, embarrassment prickling my cheeks.

Second meeting:

My wedding day

Cheeks stained black with running mascara, I stood in my street clothes between two chairs, glaring at the cursed garments I had to wear: an ivory white wedding dress with satin fixings and lace and an equally white kimono embroidered with nigh-invisible bleached cranes. They draped over the backs of each chair like the dead and gutted hides of a pure animal.

A heavy hand settled on my shoulder, and I nearly jumped out of my skin. Furiously sniffling and rubbing my eyes, I turned, expecting my husband--only to be confronted by the demon, his lizard-like hands cradling a half-eaten cut of cornbread.

"You're not supposed to be here," I said.

"Relax." Then, as though sensing my disdain at his crime, he crammed another mouthful of bread into his gob. "Stole it off the catering cart. Want some?"

"No. Get out."

"I can't just leave a bride crying in her dressing room, Nao." He adjusted his bow-tie, adorning it with a smattering of crumbs. "Why aren't you dressed?"

Because seeing both dresses laid out before me reminded me of my split culture? Because I can't disappear into the white fabric of the dress nor wear the pasty white makeup the kimono requires without accenting my darker features? Because it feels like I have to choose one culture over the other? What would a demon know, anyway?

"You okay?"

"I don't know." I sat on the floor, refusing to look at his pallid complexion and brows furrowing in infuriating confusion. "I guess it feels like I'm being forced to choose between two things that don't fully make sense and one thing I thought I was so sure of."

"It's tradition to wear multiple dresses."

"But why this dress?" An accusing finger directed at the western-style wedding dress pointed my ire.

"It's still a tradition, even between Japanese people who don't have the culture behind it. Didn't you pick it out yourself? Your husband is excited to see you in it, too, you know."

My eyes dropped to the floor where a twisting pattern of gray and red in the carpet seemed to suck my soul right into them. I could be there, between the patterns, pounding at teardrop bars, screaming, and nobody would hear me. Maybe it would be safer to lock myself away.

"Do you just want to wear the kimono?"

I shook my head. "It's not about the dresses. Am I doing right by myself, marrying a..." My eyes began to wet again. "A..."

The demon smiled. His teeth glistened as though drinking in my misery. "Another *hāfu*?" He laughed. "*Uma wa umadzure*--horses prefer the company of horses, Nao."

"Birds of a feather flock together," I translated into English, heat tipping my tongue. "That doesn't mean I can't think about everyone who would expect something like that from... someone like me. And be ashamed by it. Does that make me a horrible person?"

"No. Those thoughts really define you. A zigzagging paper *shide*, Japanese, in all respects."

I glanced at both dresses again; the demon cradled his head in one hand, sucking in a slow breath between the gap in his fangs.

"You're torn between two things," he said, "but not entirely. You speak your mother's language, but you know less of her country than your own. That makes you Japanese with a few perks."

"Does it?" I narrowed my eyes.

"Teenage mutant ninja what?"

I shrugged. "*Kōga*?"

"Turtles, Nao. Your mother would say that without a beat. But could she name all the ninja clans of Japan?"

"Probably not."

"Japanese with a few perks." The demon winked at me then indicated the dresses. "Your husband wouldn't appreciate you doubting your marriage, you know."

"I wish I could walk confidently between two cultures as he does."

"So do it. You eat curry and rice, but you aren't Indian. You drive a Mercedes, but you aren't German. Cultures merge and cultures change. There's no shame in being a part of two different cultures. Nor choosing the best parts of several others to make them your own."

"Because--"

"Because struggling with the choice is what makes you, you, isn't it?"

"It gives me the chance to still be unsure. To still choose the path that's right for me."

"Nao, you don't have to choose anything. Just be you."

"What about your choice to live in your world or ours?"

"To hell with choosing in which world. I chose to live. You did, too, Nao."

I hugged myself, pulling on my sleeve to hide a ragged scar on one wrist.

The demon knelt by me and placed a soft hand over mine. "By forgiving our wrong choices and extending love to all will rid our mind of evil and thoughts of separation. It's not you against yourself, Nao. Or us against them."

"It feels like it is."

"It does, sometimes. Let them think their thoughts and live in their world. But shine your love upon them, anyway. Isn't that what your little man on the cross tells you to do? Shine into the darkness so that you may wake from dreaming a nightmare of life."

My cheeks again prickled with tears.

"I can stop this marriage if you desire. Right now, with a snap of my fingers." He held up his saw-toothed index finger. "If you need more time--"

"No," I shook my head, then stood and snatched up the wedding dress. "Getting married is the only thing I truly feel sure about. This one?"

The demon laughed, then picked up the kimono and draped it over my empty forearm. "The duality of life is in your arms, Nao. If you focus too hard, you will only see a single point."

Third meeting:

Now

The demon cleared his throat, his muffled footsteps in the snow slowing. "And the third meeting?"

"Right here. Right now. You, the cold, and the lake."

He glanced out toward the island in the center of the lake, where a spindly cherry tree craned upward, stretching its crooked trunk toward the sky, catching snowflakes. "So, you need me to help you understand one more thing."

"No. I need you to understand."

The demon cocked his head; snow crystals fluttered to his shoulder.

"I've had a hard time understanding what I am. It's given me great pain."

"A pain we both share, as you know."

I nodded. "Pain is like *kintsugi*, filling in the cracks of a broken bowl with gold, creating something altogether whole, but shattered on the inside."

"But more beautiful than before the bowl was broken in the first place. And stronger, too, Nao."

I smiled. "I guess you already understand."

"I might, but I'm not in your head, you know. All I know is that pain hurts, but how we deal with it becomes our inner strength. And we all deal with it differently. Because we're all different, no matter the color of our skin or where we were born and raised."

"We are against a world that holds hopelessness and hope, ignorance and knowledge, happiness and sorrow. Love and hate."

"Darkness and light." His gaze centered again on the cherry tree.

I stopped and tilted my head up, letting the falling snow melt on my face. "If I focus too much on one thing, like whether I am Japanese or American, or something else entirely, the pressure of all my other choices becomes too much to bear." I took the demon's hand in mine.

He squeezed tight. "Nao, you know I've always said--"

"Be both. But I can't. The choice of one or the other makes me, me. I understand now. And I want you to as well. I don't have to be Japanese. I don't have to be American. Or both. Or neither. I can be Japanese. Or American. Or both. Or neither. I can always choose whenever I want, anytime I want. I don't have to be defined by what I am, because I can always change what that is."

"Are you avoiding choosing?"

"No. My choice is that I don't have one, and that makes me strong."

A grin gnarled up the demon's face.

"I hated Japan for so many years. Until I saw it as part of *me*, not as something to strive *for*. Or an adversary. That's why you and I are different. I am not bound by trying to live in two cultures or worlds at the same time. If I want fish for breakfast, I'm having fish. If someone chides me in English, I'll give them snark right back. If someone calls me foreign in my own land, I can just smile. Because I know what I can be. And that's ever-changing."

The demon's hand slipped out of mine, and his features melted from sharp and ragged, returning to the soft, confident tones of my husband. "Figuring this thing out they call *hāfu* is so difficult. I'm glad I could spend so many years with you working through what it means. But I must ask, what spurred your sudden answer, Nao?"

"Cornbread. For our grandchildren. I want them to know *what* they are before they start to question *who* they are. Because, ultimately, knowing *who* they are takes a lifetime. Knowing what they are shouldn't."

"And what will you tell them?"

"That they're beautiful. And that even if the blood flowing in them is different, they are Japanese." I winked at my husband. "With a few perks."

"I'll take those perks, too." He held out his hand for another piece of bread, which I gladly offered.

He paused, the cornbread halfway to his mouth, glancing at his white skin peeking out from underneath his down jacket sleeve. He pushed his sleeve back to reveal his skin and the faded, almost invisible scars crisscrossing his wrist, then scarfed down the bread.

"You'll catch a cold."

"Maybe. But I'm choosing not to hide anymore, either." He laughed. "It feels good to get rid of that demon, doesn't it?"

I laughed with him. "It'll be back when doubts creep up on me. Besides, everyone is married to their demons. Only ours can smile back."

Snowed In

By Rhea McCarthy

October 14th, Arrival, Afternoon.

We made it to the cabin with no trouble and luckily with little of the perma-snow getting into our boots. Using a stump as a make-shift seat-- while pine needles try to find their way into every crevice of my clothes-- I can see what Jed meant when he said that everything is clearer when you're up here. The sun pierces through the clouds and illuminates everything around us, enhancing the changing color of the leaves, the branches on the ground and even turns the grayness of rocks into a happier hue. The air is colder up here, but that just seems to make it more bracing. Wind whistles through your clothes and grasps at you, almost like an embrace, so pure that it seems to get rid of all negative thoughts, even ones that you don't fully feel like you could ever forget.

The snow provides the canvas, the nature provides the color is what I feel like you would say if you were here.

Jed, the park ranger, hiker extraordinaire, adventure guru know-it-all as it is, already told me all of this in his long ass speeches about how beautiful the location is,, how I must "pack warm" and "layer up," but I'll be damned if I give him the satisfaction of saying that he is right. He is also currently hollering at me to get off my ass and help him unpack the sleigh. Crates need to be unloaded, food put away and blah blah blah.

I still don't think it is enough food for two weeks, but again, he is the know-it-all, so who am I to judge his extreme wisdom?

I was never the adventurous type, I barely got to First Class in Boy Scouts before throwing in the towel; I still don't know how Jed convinced me to come out here. But at least the area is beautiful, and journaling to you may help me pass the time, or at least keep me sane.

October 14th, Night.

I thought the sun itself was beautiful, but that sunset was something else. Violets and oranges that you just can't get in the city.

We got everything unpacked into the cabin, our food supply just perfectly fills up the kitchen, looks like Jed was right again, might even have to admit that I was wrong. Sometimes I wonder if I ever had a correct thought in my head, you and Jed always seem to prove that everything I say or think is wrong.

The cabin is beautiful. If you were here, I know you would absolutely adore it. It's entirely made out of logs from the surrounding trees. Consists of two stories, the first floor being dedicated with a seating area that contains a fireplace, a fully decked out kitchen, a dining table, and a bookcase filled with books about wilderness survival, boring info about the flora and fauna and even more boring info about the location.

Upstairs is smaller, but still just as nice. It's a half floor, with a small little hallway/banister that allows you to look at the floor below. The only actual room up there is the bedroom, but with its queen-size bed, wicker chairs and window that faces the east, it more than makes up for being the only thing upstairs.

I'm also glad that I decided to bring more jackets and blankets than Jed said I needed, it's bloody colder than I was expecting. We have propane heaters, and a fireplace in the sitting area stockpiled with God knows how much wood, and an axe to go out and chop more, but even that doesn't seem to combat the chill that has begun to seep into my bones. Wood floors and walls look nice, but would it have killed them to add SOME carpet!? Anything to add some dormant heat in this place?

Jed is taking the room, leaving me with the couch. I asked Jed if we should sleep in the same bed to preserve body heat. He hit me, I think I deserved it.

October 15th, Morning.

Morning arrived earlier than I expected, and earlier than I wanted it to be. I'm not a monk, this rising-with-the-sun shit is not for me. Luckily Jed was already up and made me a cup of coffee, its smell waking me before he could. I'm starting to think he actually cares for me, or maybe he just doesn't want to deal with cranky morning me. It's probably the latter. He probably remembers pre-coffee me from when we were freshman roommates, but still, it's the thought that counts.

No real plans for the day. Jed wants to hike around and show me the area. We are bringing the .22s in case we come across any small game. I think that's the real reason we're hiking; Jed needs to shoot something and he wants me to share in the experience of killing small rodents. I think coming with him is a bad idea, I'm more likely to shoot him than the game, but my cries don't sway him. I asked Jed if he could just shoot me instead. I don't think he appreciated that, probably still thinks that it is "too soon," considering what had happened, considering it's the reason we are up here. I know you would have liked it though.

October 15th, Afternoon.

No luck with any game, but the area sure was pretty.

October 16th, Night.

We've only been up here for two days, yet I'm already bored. Sure the area is pretty and nice to walk around, but that's pretty much it. Jed has me playing card games with him once the sun goes down, but it's not like there are a lot of games that you can play with just two people, and after my upteenth game of Go-Fish, I finally addressed these frustrations to Jed. He just scoffed at me though. Boring is good, he says. Boring means that nothing is going on, and that means there is nothing we have to worry about. He may like boring, and maybe I am just a city-slicker, but I could go for some excitement. I know all of this would be easier if you were here though, but writing these feels like I am talking to you, like you are actually here, which is the best I can get right now.

But I'll take anything.

October 17th, Morning.

It feels like the days are beginning to get colder, and the clouds look heavier than they should; it seems like night is refusing to give way to day. Jed says there is nothing to worry about, that I've spent too long reading the books in the cabin and am just getting scared of stuff that I don't fully understand. Apparently it's just regular mountain weather, and I quote him here, "Nothing to get my panties in a twist about."

I really can't help but worry though, I'm getting the same sense of foreboding I got when… you left, the feeling of being in the eye of the storm, where everything is calm, right before the rain blinds you and pulls you in to drown.

I wish you were here, I know you could ease my nerves better than Jed ever could.

October 17th.

Snow has started to fall. Jed still says it is okay, but I think I see a small glimmer of worry in his eye every time he turns away from looking through the window.

October 18th

Two feet! Two feet of snow, according to Jed's estimation. He says that it's fine. Mid-Autumn snows like this are apparently common up here, the books that I love so much (according to him) say the same thing. Plus, a little extra snow never hurt anyone according to him. I don't know how he could call this "little". The clouds haven't let up either.

I asked Jed if we should cut the trip short, but I am still being told not to worry. We can still get off the mountain anytime we want, and while we may get more today, it won't last long. He also claims that while he could get down right now, I would not be able to easily trek down the mountain while walking on two feet of snow. And if I cared to read the books a little bit more than I cared to bitch, I would also see that the snow will melt just as quickly as it came. I hope he is right about this all, but I'm starting to doubt it.

October 18th

The snow started back up again. Jed still says that it is fine. I've started to read any book now that mentions the snow, or survival in the snow. It isn't doing anything to alleviate my fears.

October 19th

24 hours later and the snow still hasn't stopped. My worry is turning into panic, and Jed isn't masking his worry anymore, I can feel his nerves penetrating around the cabin, washing over me like a

wave, colder than the snow. He says everything is fine, but I know he doesn't believe it himself, that it's just some line he thinks he has to sprout for my benefit, even though I was the one who brought up the concern in the first place. He's also begun to pace around the cabin, and I think he is muttering something to himself, or planning something by himself.

The wind is also beginning to start up again, and whenever I go outside to use the outhouse it won't embrace me like it used to, instead I can hear it in my thoughts, whistling its sweet melody in my brain, whistling like you used to do.

October 21st

The wind has picked up and, surprise, the snow hasn't stopped. Jed advised that we begin to ration food. When asked if it was possible that we just leave everything and get off this forsaken mountain, he said "no". The storm would impact our vision and we may never find our way down. Plus with how cold it's getting and how slow moving it would be, we wouldn't be able to get down before night, and who knows what hypothermia or other cold-related afflictions will we get when the sun goes down.

I snapped, told him that we should have gotten off this mountain earlier, to which Jed replied by locking himself in the bedroom. I don't give a fuck about his hurt feelings though. I know I'm right, and through the whistling of the wind, I hear you agree with me.

October 22nd? Maybe the 23rd

I can feel you in my mind more now, the whispers that I heard before have changed to full words, spoken in your voice. Maybe it's just an echo of you, me clinging to your remnants so I have someone to talk to, someone to bounce ideas off of, someone to keep me sane.

I can tell that you're not always here, sometimes you leave, and no matter how much I call, you don't respond. Even when you are here, I feel like you can't hear me, even when I speak aloud, but I can hear you. But while I can't see you, I know you can see me. This journal is proof of it. Everything I write in it, you respond. Maybe it has taken the shape of a reverse Ouija board, one where you speak, and I write.

Maybe I really am going insane.

I can tell that Jed doesn't like the fact that I continue to write in this journal, he scoffs every time I pick it up. But with how much time he is spending up in his room now, those scoffs are few and far between. Even if we couldn't communicate with it, I know I would keep doing it, just to piss him off, because even though he is one of the last people I could imagine wanting to see right now, he is the only person I can see right now, and bitter scoffs are better than no human interaction in my opinion. Plus, he got us into this situation, he can deal with my journaling.

What do you think?

Yeah, I thought so.

I've Lost Count

The snowfall has stopped, but we are still in no condition to go anywhere. It is piled so high that we can barely walk through it. This morning I think the door was actually frozen shut, it took Jed banging against it multiple times to finally open up, and his efforts were rewarded with a wall of snow. We can still get to the outhouse, but only barely. And if a 100-foot walk takes minutes, I can only imagine what going down the mountain would be like.

Food is running low; I don't know how much longer it will last. Wood supply is also running low, and due to the snow, we are in no position, nor even have the morale, to chop down more.

Two more inches of snow, because apparently we didn't already have enough

I agree, this is all Jed's fault. He is the one who wanted us up here. He is the one who didn't take us down when it started getting bad. He is the one who didn't pack enough fucking food. And now with the snow starting up again for the ump-teenth time, who knows when we will get off this fucking mountain.

Oh, and this even harsher rationing of food, where does Jed get the balls. We only have three days left of food if we continue with half rations he says, but I don't buy it. We had at least a week left of food if we ate at a normal pace when the ration started, how are we already down to three days of food at half rations. I've only been eating half rations, how are we down this far?

No, Jed wouldn't be eating more of his share, he can't be. He's an ass, sure, but he is better at this than I am. He wouldn't break the ration rule, even if it would spite me. You're wrong, you have to be wrong.

But are you?

Where are you going?

I think I can see you, out in the snow. You're always out of sight, and always leave right after I see you , but it has to be you. I don't understand why you're out there, maybe you're finding us a path so we can get off this mountain, maybe you're just embracing the weather, you always did love the cold. We can leave Jed behind, he deserves it. I hope you get back here soon though, we can't talk if you're not here reading this, and I miss you.

I can feel my stomach eating itself

I am so hungry, I don't remember the last time I ate, when the food ran out. Do you remember?

I thought so.

Jed is jealous of us, I can still see it when he looks over here, he is just mad that he doesn't have a wife by his side, someone that would be by his side even after their death, mad that he doesn't have anyone to talk to. It's not my fault he stopped talking to me, I tried. Its not my fault that he is so fucking uptight. That he spends more time in the woods than with his wife. It's not my fault that she left him. We've tried talking to him, you know we have. But every time we speak up, he just looks away. When you were away, I tried to go into the room, I swear I did, but he wouldn't open the fucking door.

Oh? You were able to go up there when I was asleep? What did you guys talk about? What do you mean you guys didn't talk?

What do you mean he was hiding something?

What cans?

The day (and night) of splattered blood

I did what I had to do right? You agree with me, it was justified. I did what had to be done, no one can fault me on that. He deserved it.

He was smuggling food. I knew that we weren't running out of food that quickly, that we couldn't have been going through the rations, that ration that he implemented, that fast. You were the one who told me that he was hiding food from me. You have to realize what my reaction would have been when I found out you were right. Bags of beef jerky, cans of chili, some oranges, all tuck away, out of sight and out of mind, in a room he locked me out of, since the beginning.

He never wanted me in that room, even during the first day. I was condemned down to the couch, while he slept like a king, all tucked away from the lowly peasant that he must've thought I was. Was this the plan all along? Finally grew tired of me weeping about you, so he decides to bring me up here and starve me out, as some sort of sick, slow killing torture?

You weren't here for this obviously, you were out there again, trying to find a path down I'm sure, but you must have known how I felt. He tried to defend himself, that it was just for when things got even worse, so he could cheer me up. As if. How much worse could it get? I've been without food for days, and yet not a word from him. You told me that he was smuggling it away from me, why would I believe him when I have you.

And nobody can fault me for what happened next, it was to be expected, it was natural, survival of the fittest, retribution for my wrongs, getting rid of the weakest link. I am justified! Anyone would have done the same, you would have done the same right? You wanted this to happen right? Why else would you have told me? You always wished that I took charge more, and now I finally have.

I still don't know how the axe got into my hands. Maybe you came back and put it there, to usher me forward on what I had to do. The .22's sat in the corner, using them would have been kinder for Jed, but the axe, oh, the axe; the feel, the heft, the power in it, it was the best feeling I've had since our wedding. Yeah, the axe felt right. He screamed and screamed and screamed, so loud that you must have heard it, so intensely that it would have broken the confines of this journal, but I didn't care. He brought me up here so no one could hear my cry, and that sword can cut both ways.

I've never been one for hunting, you know this. The thought of killing another animal always made my stomach turn. I was a hypocritical carnivore. I could eat the meat, just couldn't stand to acknowledge where it came from and how it got here. But bringing that axe down rendering through flesh, was ecstasy. The blood gushed from the ruin of his arm, flying so high that it splattered into my laughing mouth, and oh, it was nice. Tasty even. He stopped pleading and tried to defend himself, but I was in control now! I would allow no quarter to be given. I brought it down, again and again! First into his other arm, then into his leg, my screams of excitement joined his scream of fear, creating a haunting melody, the perfect soundtrack to his ruin and my ascension.

Again and again I brought it down. Flesh and bones, fingers and toes flew off and around me, a perfect storm of red to forget the insufferable storm of white. I don't know when his screams stopped, all I knew was when I walked out of the room, a wealth of food items in my hands, mine never did.

Food

Oh it was a feast. Juice running down my chin, the taste of jerky in my mouth, the feeling of chili warming me up from inside my belly. His body sat slumped in the corner where I dragged it, the holes where his eyes once were watched me the entire time, but what about it. He tried to rid me of my rations, so now he got to watch me feast.

Rations are running low

I knew you wouldn't have blamed me for what happened, that you saw the justice in me killing him. And you're absolutely right about the current situation, the remaining food won't last much longer. And he is already in pieces.

It really would be a shame to leave his body

Lying there

Unused.

Rations filled back up

The snow preserved what I couldn't eat. I never knew that flesh could taste so good. The blood that sprayed into my mouth during my justice stirred up my appetite for this without me even knowing, and finally indulging myself in him, oh that was a treat. Beef could never compare. I don't know why we aren't offering this in restaurants everywhere, it's practically the same as cow; rarer, stringier, juicier cow.

I wish you could eat some, you could experience what I am tasting. Remember that fancy steakhouse that we went to for one of our anniversaries. You got the veal, you said it was the best thing that you have ever eaten, I took a bite, and I agreed with you.

This doesn't even compare. Nothing will ever compare.

Waiting

There isn't enough, not enough to last me. I need to get off this mountain, but was Jed right, was there no way off, was it still too dangerous?

No.

Jed was weak.

He succumbed to our situation, to his hunger, to my fury. He knew he couldn't get off this mountain, but I can. I have you Cecilia, you've been looking for a way off this mountain. You're out there right now. You'll find it, you'll save me.

And then, we can be together again.

Leaving

I see you out there, beckoning. Could it be possible that you found a way off this mountain, for us to be together. I can see it in your eyes, it seems like you actually can hear me. Is that true? It is!? Do I no longer need this? I've been writing in it for so long, I can see your arms, beckoning me to move faster, but I must write this down, this is how I started my journey, and it's how I want to end it too. There is no time to put on a jacket, or to put on shoes, you need me now, you'll protect me, you'll lead me away from this mountain

We can finally be together again.